THE MISSILE GAME

A DR. SCOTT JAMES THRILLER

GLENN SHEPARD

MYSTERY HOUSE

Mystery House Publishing, Inc.

Newport News, VA

ISBN 0-9905893-5-8

ISBN 978-0-9905893-5-8

Cover and interior design by Annie Biggs.

Printed in the United States of America.

THE MISSILE GAME

1

Operating Room
Scott James Surgery Center
6:41 p.m.

 THE DECISION TO OPERATE on Elizabeth Keyes was a mistake.

She refused Propofol as her anesthetic because it killed Michael Jackson, then turned down the use of the second best medication, Versed. At the end, she said she wanted an older style of anesthesia, Valium and Demerol, but in reduced doses. She claimed that she was sensitive to all sedatives.

Sure enough, it took only 2 milligrams of Valium and 50 milligrams of Demerol to knock her out. Most people required 10 milligrams of Valium and 100 milligrams of Demerol, with a little extra if they begin to wake up during the operation. Not so with Elizabeth Keyes. She slept soundly.

And kept on sleeping ...

I stood over the operating table, looking at her, waiting

3

for her to wake up, then asked, "Why's it taking her so long to recover from the anesthetic?"

Dr. Boyd Carey, my anesthesiologist, looked over his half-frame glasses and said, "If you hadn't bowed to Keyes' ridiculous demand for a particular sedative, this would have only taken forty-five minutes."

Dr. Boyd Carey was a thin vegan who probably would've been happier if he ate a burger once in a while. Fine wrinkles in his forty-five-year-old dark skin made him look sixty.

"Come on now, Boyd. Relax." I arched my back, stiff from bending over so much. After yet another twelve-hour day, I was exhausted. I'd just hit forty and I was really starting to feel it. "Hey, at least we aren't working in the tobacco fields."

"Oh God, you're not going to start in again on your stories of slaving away in the fields to pay for college—"

"I could if—"

"Please, spare me."

I removed my surgical gown and gloves, then took off my surgical cap and finger-combed my hair. Dr. Carey looked at the patient for a minute, and then said, "No. She's still sound asleep. We should have given her Propofol, like we do with all our patients. She'd be awake by now. But no. You always grant all your patients' every wish and kiss their surgically-raised asses."

That's not exactly true. Each day I look out on a waiting

room, and when I see broken pieces, I try my best to put them back together. I grew up on a farm, working in the fields. Now I am the founder of a surgery center for craniofacial reconstruction, with an emphasis on facial deformities, such as cleft lips, deformed mandibles and maxillae, and orbits that are too widely separated, or compacted.

In other words, I fix people's faces.

Dr. Carey growled, "She hasn't had enough sedation to hurt a fly. You should just go home. I'll watch her until she wakes up. At least one of us should be able to enjoy this evening."

"No. I'm not leaving until she's awake. I'll be in the waiting room. Call me and I'll be back in a second if there's a problem."

I left the operating room to look for Anna Duke, the friend who was supposed to pick up Elizabeth Keyes after surgery. Keyes was my office manager—*another* reason why operating on her was a mistake—but I didn't know Anna Duke, and there was no one in the waiting room. We had no information on her in our records, either, which was strange.

I made a quick phone call to my wife, Alicia, telling her that Keyes hadn't awakened from surgery yet, and it would be another hour before I could leave my surgery center. "Alright," she said, "do what you have to. But there's always *something* to keep you there late. The boys wanted to see you and ... I'll put the boys to sleep and keep the casserole hot in the oven," she sighed as she continued, "again."

Just as I hung the phone, I clearly heard a *thump*. I was still in the waiting room. I ran down the hall to the OR, opened the door, and saw Dr. Carey lying there. With blood on his neck. His eyes and mouth were open like he had tried to scream, but he was frozen, paralyzed.

I checked on Keyes—EKG, pulse—saw she was still sleeping, then went to work on Dr. Carey. I got on my knees next to him and checked for a pulse. There wasn't one. I jerked the stethoscope out of his jacket and listened to his chest. It was very faint, just a feeble *bump, bump, bump*. I started chest compressions. I gave him six compressions and two breaths. His heart sounds were slow and distant. I grabbed the phone and dialed 911. I said, "A man's been stabbed. He's dying. I need help. Please send an ambulance STAT."

As I waited for them to come I kept working on Carey. Within just a moment, his heart sounds were basically gone. Silence.

I remembered my stash of Valium. I had a huge quantity of Valium, over a hundred vials of liquid, plus a large number of ten-milligram tablets. Valium had been so popular as an anesthetic and the drug salesman had given me such a good price on it at the time, that I had stocked up.

But such a quantity was going to look bad when the

medics got there. I had to hide it. I grabbed the stash of Valium. For the first time in my entire surgical career, I was panic-stricken: Valium everywhere and Boyd Carey on the floor, dead, with two needle marks in his jugular.

What just happened? I was only gone for a few moments.

2

Kandahar Airfield, Afghanistan
Three Months Earlier
5:58 a.m.

EVER SINCE HE WAS seven years old, Charlie played video games. He had mastered the games almost immediately, having innately good reflexes and hand-eye coordination. He also lacked moral qualms ... about anything. After winning several gaming competitions in his late 20s, he was contacted by the Central Intelligence Agency, and accepted their offer to move from murdering virtual foes to slaughtering real ones.

The CIA granted Charlie access to a new program which involved piloting drones. Charlie learned, very quickly, to operate the robot aircraft as well as the Air Force's best pilots. His penchant for video games made his skills exceptional, and these gaming talents readily transferred to drone operation. Charlie had even proven himself to be brilliant under pressure, and once he'd tasted actual combat, he'd gained a voracious appetite for it. The thrill of killing a virtual terrorist couldn't compare to the rush of killing one made of flesh and blood.

"Alpha Charlie" was now a CIA-paid civilian contractor whose mission in Afghanistan was to control pilotless aircraft, and destroy enemy targets. He had spent the last four days glued to the monitors in the control center, even as the other eight members of the Air Force forensics team took brief meal and sleep breaks. Ninety-six hours earlier, just before he was scheduled to return to his civilian job in America, Forensics had identified the Al Qaeda leader Muhammad Bin Garza. He was only 230 miles away, in the Mir Ali area of North Waziristan. Charlie canceled his flight home. He wanted blood.

Alpha Charlie was stationed in one of two identical Quonset huts, spaced roughly fifty meters apart, on the air base. The U.S. Air Force forensics team was housed in the other hut. Their function was to get the drones airborne, to locate and identify targets, and to land the vehicles when their missions were completed.

Alpha Charlie spent most of his time sitting alone inside his own hut. He did not sit in an ordinary chair. At the end of each armrest were two joysticks, one for each hand.

"Alpha Charlie, Alpha Charlie, get ready for action. The target's on the move."

The words vibrated in Charlie's earpiece as he bolted upright and flexed his 220-pound, six-foot-two-inch frame.

It had been two years since they'd had a positive ID on Bin Garza. The notorious Al Qaeda leader was responsible for the suicide bombings in Mumbai, Amman, London, and Somalia, and had connections to the World Trade Center attack in New York. Now he was a sitting duck. He had been spotted while entering a complex of tents and adobe houses adjacent to the mountains. He would be leaving any moment now. This was the one and only chance Alpha Charlie would ever have to eliminate Bin Garza. Bin Garza's death would be the ultimate notch in his gun barrel. His job back home could wait. He had taken out terrorists before, but Bin Garza was the trophy he had been training for his whole life.

Just as Charlie was receiving the alert, Air Force Colonel Ben Edwards, director of drone operations, ran into the hut.

He glanced at Alpha Charlie's hands as they moved the joysticks. Edwards marveled at how Charlie's fingers glided over the controls and easily performed maneuvers that his other pilots struggled with.

Edwards suddenly saw the blinking red light on the fuel gauge. One hundred pounds of fuel left. Seventy-two miles of life left in the fuel tank, not enough to get the aircraft halfway back to Kandahar. "Charlie," he said, "you're running out of fuel."

The Missile Game

Alpha Charlie pretended not to hear. He had already extended the flight time five hours by using the updrafts of the mountains to conserve fuel and by lowering the aircraft's speed to 320 mph. But now he was concerned. An hour earlier, he'd ordered his Global Hawk refueled, but the airborne tanker had yet to appear on his radar screen.

His focus remained locked on the three monitors in front of him. Screen A showed a flurry of activity in the small, peaceful Haqqui tribal village. Bin Garza was going for a ride. That was it. Charlie's waiting was over. He leaned forward and watched carefully.

In the center of the village, a 1960s Mercedes sedan and a 1980s Chrysler New Yorker were parked in front of an adobe house. Alongside the two cars, a small entourage surrounded three men who had just left the house and were walking to the vehicles. A dozen cheering villagers reached out to touch the men as guards pushed them aside. On Screen B, the forensics experts focused on the faces of the men and enlarged them. Screen C showed a broad view of the five-square-mile area surrounding the target.

Screen A showed the men getting into the two cars, while screen B flipped through stills of the faces. The computer fine-tuned the quality of the images, and then Charlie heard excitement build from the other hut.

"That's definitely Bin Garza," Charlie said in a low voice.

"And that's his number two, Shakel, with him. We can get two for the price of one, if we hit 'em now."

The third man on the screen kept his shemagh pulled over his face and could not be identified.

"Alpha Charlie," Colonel Edwards said, "we have Al Qaeda's two top men together. Targets confirmed. It's now or never. Get 'em."

Alpha Charlie turned to Screen A, the target monitor that showed live pictures from the MQ-4A Global Hawk drone he controlled. This aircraft was the largest and best-equipped drone in his fleet, but it was brand new and untested. It had been airborne for nearly forty-eight hours and had circled at fifty thousand feet, filming the area where Pakistani intelligence had said the Al Qaeda operatives were staying.

Sweat dripped down Charlie's brow as he saw the plummeting fuel gauge now reading empty.

Time was running out. Charlie focused the camera, centering it on the now moving car.

A pissed off Edwards looked at Screen C. "Fuck! There's a hill! They'll disappear behind it in twenty seconds. Charlie, you gotta strike now!"

Alpha Charlie didn't respond, but he heard Edwards. He had one shot and didn't want to miss. His mental clock ticked down, *twenty, nineteen, eighteen, seventeen.* His left hand guided a blinking red target square over the car. With the image of the square fixed to the target, Charlie centered the X. He quickly touched the red trigger button with his right thumb and fired the five-foot-long missile. *Click*. The Hellfire missile locked on the Mercedes. *Seven, six, five, four* ... At a speed of 950 mph, the missile would be paying the car a surprise visit within three seconds.

But would it get there in time?

3

The Mir Ali Village, Afghanistan
6:04 a.m.

 A HIGH-PITCHED *WHIRRR*, LIKE the sound of a model airplane, filled the sky above the village. The driver of the Mercedes looked up to see the silvery flash of reflected sunlight emerging from the obscurity of the mountain behind.

As the driver accelerated, he saw the five-foot-long Hellfire missile speeding towards them. Bin Garza screamed in terror as he gripped the seat of the car and braced himself. The explosion was tremendous, ripping the men and car to pieces.

One hundred feet away, the unidentified man in the shemagh, Omar Farok, felt his Chrysler bounce around like a toy ball. The concussion of the impact nearly deafened him. He watched from the Chrysler as a fireball swallowed up the Mercedes, followed only by a blinding cloud of smoke and dirt.

The Missile Game

Fortunately for Farok, his driver was familiar with the terrain of the village and the Chrysler instantly turned left onto a mountain path, dodging around trees. As the Chrysler slammed to a halt, a terrified Farok dove out of the car and ran into a mountain cave. He sat trembling as he watched another Hellfire missile devour the Chrysler in a ball of red flames.

Farok's driver staggered into the cave. His face had been blackened by the flames and his clothes nearly ripped from his body. Farok stood and walked to him. "We alone survive. We are going to turn away from Al Qaeda. You will help me as we merge with the Islamic State in Levant. Our state is Iraq and Syria. The caliphate. The Islamic State in Iraq and Syria. ISIS is the new direction."

The driver's eyes widened as he looked at Farok. "But Bin Garza directed Shakel and you to continue to pursue a moderate course with Al Qaeda. To steer from the brutality of ISIS. To gain the confidence of the people we control by treating them like our own family."

Farok's fists knotted. "You know I spoke in opposition to his gestures of kindness to the people in Bin Garza's control. A true leader is strong and gains respect by making people fearful of his vengeance, as God invokes the fear in all of us. Strict discipline is the new direction of our Islamic State. I will slay all who disobey me."

"You cannot disobey Bin Garza's directive. We must

continue on in Al Qaeda," the haggard driver said. "And I will fight your disobedience."

Farok jerked a pistol from his shemagh and fired five shots. His driver fell to the dirt. His mouth opened to speak, but his head fell slowly to one side before words came out. Farok shot him three more times, then shouted, "God tells me to join the Islamic State! I will dispense with Bin Garza's weakness!" He looked upward. "Allah, I swear on your blessed name, I will make the American pigs quake in fear of me."

Kandahar Airfield, Afghanistan
6:05 a.m.

Colonel Edwards and the forensics team cheered.

Alpha Charlie did not celebrate, even as the refueling aircraft came in and saved his drone from sputtering to the earth on its last pound of fuel. He was pleased about the millions that he had made from this kill. The extra money would allow him to shift his drone control station and missiles back home and continue his missions from there, but still, he wasn't about to jump up and down and cheer. He'd done his job.

He stood as bottles of Dom Perignon were uncorked. Without fanfare, Charlie grabbed a drink and downed it. Then he poured himself another. As he swallowed, he thought to himself, "All in a day's work."

4

ICU, Jackson City Hospital
Jackson City, North Carolina
7:16 a.m.

 Resuscitative attempts on Dr. Carey had failed, even though the paramedics had labored over him for an hour.

After that, I'd been up all night, going between the police station for questioning and the hospital to check on Elizabeth Keyes. She'd been transferred from my surgery center to Jackson City Hospital, and even after twelve hours she still hadn't awakened from her surgery, which concerned me. I had recounted in my mind every detail of the procedure on Keyes but I couldn't think of anything that had gone wrong.

The surgery had gone smoothly. It wasn't a big deal. I wasn't reconstructing an accident victim's entire face—this was just a routine cosmetic procedure. I'd placed silicone implants in Elizabeth Keyes' cheeks and chin and had taken a little fat from her neck. I didn't think she really needed any of this done. She was beautiful before surgery. I did it because she insisted. But it was just a minor thing—nothing to it. The procedures I'd done on her didn't even require bandages, and generated little bruising.

But I stood now in the ICU and took in the whole nightmare. I almost felt like breaking down and crying. Boyd Carey was dead. And Keyes wasn't waking up. I couldn't believe what had happened.

I again called my wife. "They haven't done the autopsy," I said to her, "but it's definitely a homicide. Someone jabbed a needle into Carey's neck, and probably shot him with a big bolus of a drug. It might take a few days to resolve all this."

"Who … ?" Her voice was suspicious. "Why would someone … *kill* … Dr. Carey?"

"I don't know"

"Who … ?" She paused. "You should have just kept doing your surgery at the hospital. You should have never spent all that money building your own surgery center. And operating on that girl in your office … *after hours*. Is there something going on between the two of you?"

"Alicia—please … You know there's nothing between us, or between me and anyone."

"I know that? No. I don't know what you've been doing at the office late every night. Maybe this explains a lot of things."

"Please believe me Alicia. I've never lied to you."

Alicia didn't respond.

"Please believe me"

"Hmmp. I hope everything works out at the hospital. I mean, you'll need to still see patients and operate even though your office is closed ... I need money to pay all the bills."

"I know."

She hung up. I called her back twice and even texted her, but she didn't respond.

I did not want to hear that.

Regardless, I went back to Keyes' bedside and waited.

I'd been dealing with the police almost constantly since Dr. Carey's death, but none of that had really meant anything. It was just a prologue. I knew it was only a matter of time before I would have to talk to Harris—Detective Sergeant Pete Harris. He and I had always been on friendly terms. Until now.

Harris nodded to me as he walked into the ICU. He strolled up and stood at Elizabeth Keyes' bedside. Harris was wearing his orange-and-brown-checkered sport coat and his usual embroidered western shirt, with string tie. He never used his police uniform. Harris' father, "Pop" Harris, had been a cop in town and always treated his son as he would a police academy student. His dad taught him that, "It's a cop's job to see things that other people miss." Pete

benefited from his father's teachings when he attended
the Police Academy. While his high school grades were
marginal, he made straight A's in the Academy.

He was offered a job first with the Raleigh Police
Department, about twenty miles away, then offered one at
Chapel Hill, which was slightly closer, turned them both
down, and took a job on the Jackson City Police force,
instead. His promotions came quickly. With just eight years
under his belt, he was asked to be police chief, a job he
turned down. Despite the large salary differential between
the two positions, he kept his rank and his job just as it was.
All he wanted to be was a homicide detective.

There was a long period of silence as Harris considered
his words before speaking. He looked at me through slits of
eyes narrowed by thick, bushy eyebrows and heavy eyelids
that gave him the look of a bulldog. He was a large man, six-
foot-one-inch tall and, though muscular, was overweight
at 264 pounds. In a low, gravelly voice, he said, clearing
his throat first, "Ahem … You know anything about Doc
Carey's death?"

He stared at me until I looked away. His look was
accusatory. I hadn't done anything wrong. "As I said last
night, I heard an odd noise —"

"Why don't you just step over here with me."

I followed Harris out of the privacy curtains and to the
reception area. "Now," he said, "what were you saying?"

"We had just finished operating on Keyes."

"This is you and Dr. Carey."

"Yes. It was just the two of us. We were operating on Keyes. We were waiting for her to wake up from sedation."

I told him about the whole incident, the loud thumping noise of the body hitting the floor, my attempts to save Dr. Carey, as well as the reason I hadn't been in the OR when the murder occurred.

Harris asked, in a quiet, calm tone, "Do you know this Duke woman? Is she a member of your staff?"

"Anna Duke? No. I've never met her. Of course, Elizabeth Keyes is my office manager. But I don't know Anna Duke. And there was no record of her in the patient's files, either, which is kind of strange. Anyway, she wasn't there."

"Well," Harris said, "the two needle marks in Dr. Carey's neck are tellin' me drugs were injected by the killer. Someone with 'nough medical skill ta hit the big artery." He paused as he stared at me. I was really uncomfortable. I didn't want to be there.

A man wearing a white lab coat over police-issued black trousers and shoes ran down the hallway toward Harris. He stopped short of the detective and said, as he breathed hard from his exertion, "Mr. Harris, I have to see you right away."

Harris and the police lab technician huddled in a corner, and I was alone again with my thoughts.

5

BBC/World News
11:06 GMT/UTC

 A SPOKESMAN FOR THE Islamic State in Iraq and Syria, ISIS, is claiming responsibility for the bombing of the offices of an American defense contractor in Abu Dahbi on Sunday. A spokesman for the group called the office "a control center for American drones." American officials have repeatedly denied using civilian contractors to operate missile-firing drones. The Brookings Institution released a report on Tuesday accusing the U.S. Government of operating so-called "black sites," or secret drone control centers, inside the United States. The U.S. State Department, addressing accusations of the existence of drone-operating black sites inside the U.S., said, in a prepared statement, "Those types of rumors are extremely irresponsible."

Drone Control Center, "Alpha Charlie"
United States
3:04 a.m.

In a small, dimly lit room, Charlie turned his attention to the thickly padded executive office chair, still in its factory wrappings. He stripped the bubble wrap and neatly folded and stuffed it in the trash. The chair tilted in all directions. The two armrests were fourteen inches wide and featured dials, black plastic knobs, and detachable control handles. He sat in the chair and twisted his body all around. It leaned back too much and not far enough to the right. Manipulation of control buttons on the chair arms corrected these problems.

He leaned from side to side and adjusted the comfort panels on the seat and back. Lifting two heavy rubber handles, grooved to fit his fingers and thumbs, he touched the rounded tops, and activated his computer screens. The two hand pieces were magnetically held to the armrests but otherwise had no restrictive attachments. He moved his arms in every imaginable position and touched each finger to its own control. Every finger touchpad activated controls on the screen and boxes that magnified sections of the landscape on the primary screen.

With activation of this sophisticated control system, his drones were responsive to his every command.

Charlie surveyed the three computer screens attached to the Broad Area Maritime Surveillance, Unmanned Aircraft

System (BAMS/UAS) workstation. He put on a head set with half-inch earphones and a quarter-inch microphone on the end of a thin wire. He flipped the switch and began to talk. "Colonel Edwards, are you with me?"

"Yes sir, Alpha Charlie."

"Do we have a secure vocal transmission?"

"That's an affirmative, sir. The audios are so protected, the only people that know they exist are our aircraft crews in Kandahar, and Creech Air Force base in Nevada."

"Do I have control of everything now?"

"You're A-OK to go from there. Your new chair is connected to everything now, your Global Hawks, the Reapers, and your Predators."

6

Trenton, New Jersey
10:15 a.m.

NICOLE BANZAR'S FATHER PURCHASED the missiles when they were decommissioned from Russian service, after the 1987 Nuclear Disarmament Treaty. Since then they'd been stored in a warehouse at the end of a pot-hole infested road, lost in rows of other old warehouses.

A week earlier, Nicole Banzar had received a five-word text: TARGET IS SOUTH OF YOU.

Her reply had been, simply: UNDERSTOOD. SEND HELP.

She'd quickly recruited eight "soldiers," most of them from a Chicago Al Qaeda splinter group eager to get into some "real action." If she were able to assemble maybe five more, she would have thirteen—maybe fifteen, if she got lucky—soldiers and operatives for the attack against Alpha Charlie.

To prepare for the operation, she'd sent four men ahead of her to the warehouse.

The Missile Game

*　*　*

A rusted Chevy truck filled with four uncomfortable-looking men made a path through the high weeds that had taken over the crumbling parking lot. The pickup stopped at a building with flaking paint and an old rusty sign that said, "Property of J.J. Hussam Import Furniture."

The four men didn't give a damn about the doors of the place. They weren't coming back. Using crowbars, they tore off the heavy boards that had been nailed across the front of the warehouse and drove their truck into the building. Twenty, tarp-covered boxes and a dusty tractor-trailer were sitting alone in the large empty space.

The four men quickly exposed the boxes and took inventory. One grabbed a toolbox from the pickup and lifted the hood of the vintage Mack truck. Another carried two, five-gallon containers of diesel fuel to the truck's cylindrical tanks and began refueling. A message was quickly texted, and soon a Pontiac Grand Prix with dented fenders and crackled blue paint drove in behind the pickup. Two men in dungarees and soiled white T-shirts got out, followed by Nicole Banzar.

Nicole had tousled black hair, big brown eyes, and wore tight black jeans that hugged her long legs and slim hips.

A pink camisole contained her full bust, but her age was belied by fine lines on the deeply tanned skin of her face and arms.

Nicole's soldiers began loading the heavy boxes on the truck. Their voices echoed in the large building. Nicole knelt beside a stack of six boxes, all of them covered in Chinese lettering. Only two words were written in English, in a position where the sender would be listed: Astana, Kazakhstan. Inside, lay the parts for a Silkworm missile.

7

ICU, Jackson City Hospital
Jackson City, North Carolina
11:15 a.m.

 THE ICU WAS STARTING to come to life. More people were coming and going as another busy day was in full swing. Keyes was finally awake, which made me feel better. She'd been out for a long time.

I still hadn't had a wink of sleep. I stood at the nurse's station, propped up, while Harris stood off to one side, talking on the phone to his people, going over the details of the previous night.

Standing there, I was suddenly overcome by the very strong feeling that there was something going on with my patient, but I was worn out, fuzzy, and wasn't sure what to think. I could hear an attendant back there, talking to her. "Here, honey," he seemed to say, "Take these pills. You'll feel better."

The attendant suddenly slipped through the parted

privacy curtains and then walked out the door. He was an enormous man, gigantic, with a blond ponytail. His sudden appearance and disappearance definitely caught my attention, and though I was still unsure about what was going on, I called to the nearby attending nurse to follow me in to check on Keyes.

We parted the curtains and started to run our typical checks. I took Keyes' pulse. It was slow, only forty-eight. I tried to awaken her. She didn't respond. Her breathing became slower, as did her pulse. I shook her shoulder to arouse her. No response. Something was wrong. I looked at the vitals screen: Her oxygen was only 80 percent, her blood pressure a dangerously low seventy-over-thirty. Her skin was gray. Keyes was in trouble.

I threw back the privacy curtains and shouted, "Where's this patient's ICU doctor?"

The doctor in charge of the ICU, Stewart, and two nurses, came immediately.

"When I was here an hour ago, my patient was awake and talking to me. Now, she's totally unresponsive. What's going on?"

"I don't know," Stewart answered. "When I checked her thirty minutes ago, she was responsive and her vitals were normal."

"Why the hell didn't the attendant who was just in here notice this patient was decompensating?"

"Which attendant?"

I looked around but didn't see him.

Stewart called the head nurse on duty. I described to her as best I could the person I'd seen leaving Keyes' room just as I'd arrived: tall, muscular, wearing green scrubs, a surgical mask, and having a blond tail of hair hanging down.

"Not one of mine," she said. "I haven't seen anyone like that here today—or ever."

Stewart turned to me and through clenched teeth said, "Maybe the real question here is: What did you smack her with in your surgery center? It must've been potent stuff to last this long."

"What did her drug screen show when she came in last night?"

Dr. Stewart pulled Keyes' chart from the rack at the foot of the bed. "Hmm. You're right. The nurse's reports show she 'came around' after admission. Toxicology shows she had only a trace of Demerol and no Valium upon arrival, certainly not enough to do anything but make her a little groggy."

"I know. What medications has she been given since then?"

"Absolutely none. She's received no medication from this hospital since being admitted last night," Stewart responded.

Then, frowning, he looked me in the eyes and said,

"This patient was just fine a little while ago. What'd you do, give her something strong to shut her up?"

I resisted the urge to tell him to go screw himself. Instead, I appealed to his sense of reason. "Look, forget the finger-pointing and let's help her. She's in trouble. She's overdosed on something or there's something else going on here; this is not a delayed reaction to yesterday's meds. Repeat those blood studies. Check her out neurologically. Rule out a cerebral vascular accident. And find that tall male attendant with blond hair. He might have given her something."

The commotion had aroused Harris, who had come over to see what the problem was. Dr. Stewart looked at me and then at Keyes, and his expression changed. I could tell that he, too, sensed that something wasn't right. He took his stethoscope from his neck, moved it over her chest and then the carotid arteries. With his ophthalmoscope, Stewart looked through her pupils to the inside of her eyes. After testing her reflexes with his rubber mallet, he yelled across the room to the charge nurse, "Call the blood lab STAT and send for X-ray. I need a portable skull X-ray."

He raised the top of Keyes' bed until she was at a forty-five-degree sitting position, increased the nasal oxygen to 100 percent, and upped the IV fluid rate to 300 cc an hour.

Stewart turned to me. "Something's neurologically wrong."

"Like what?"

"She's either strokin' or somebody shot her up with drugs."

Harris looked at me and said, "Miss Keyes' blood on admission showed only traces of the two drugs you gave her in surgery."

"Well, actually, I didn't give her anything. Dr. Carey administered all the drugs."

"Dr. Stewart is saying somebody's pumped her up with drugs since she's been here."

He paused for an excruciating five seconds, then said, "Dr. James, did ya give that to her?"

"Of course not! Why would I want to harm her?"

"What the hell's going on around here, Dr. James?" Harris asked.

"I don't know! Listen, we need to clear out. Give the ICU staff a chance to do their job."

We stepped away from Keyes. I said, "Pete, I don't know what's going on. Honestly."

He cleared his throat—one of his "ahems," then said, "My men found a load of Valium in your office, and some of it dropped on the floor like 'someone' was in a hurry to hide it. Valium. The same stuff in your nurse's blood. And I'm guessin' we'll find it in Dr. Carey."

I flushed all over. Buying all that Valium was a mistake. I shook my head. "I bought it over six months ago. It was cheap and I used a lot back then. But I *did not* use any of it on Keyes or Carey. You gotta' believe me."

Harris "ahemed" and stared at me until I had to look away.

Why did I feel guilty? Buying drugs for surgical procedures is certainly no crime. But Harris was making it one.

"Listen, Pete, I have to go back to my surgery center to get my files—"

"What files?"

"I have lots of patients in and out of the hospital that I have to care for. I need their records—"

"Alright. Okay. I'll tell my man over there to let you in. But we need to talk more."

"No problem."

"Do not go into your OR—when you're over there—for any reason whatsoever. That's now a crime scene."

8

ABC NEWS/ONLINE

 LYON, FRANCE: The Minister of The Interior has called for an international investigation into the suicide-bombing of The Littleton Company. Officials in Lyon and Paris have confirmed that the bomb blast last week revealed the existence of "an extensive electronic control facility." French officials believe the complex was being used by The Littleton Company, a civilian defense contractor, to operate military drones. Littleton has extensive connections with U.S. drone operations, including a variety of operations contracts. Littleton Company CEO, Richard Pratt, himself a retired Air Force colonel, cited confidentiality agreements with the Air Force in refusing to comment. The small, unimpressive office complex is located in Corbas, a suburb of Lyon. U.S. Department of Defense Officials have repeatedly stated that no such drone control "black sites"

exist, and have been adamant in squashing reports of the existence of civilian control centers on U.S. soil.

Edenton, North Carolina
3:30 p.m.

Nicole Banzar had recruited Michelle to be one of the "soldiers." Michelle was twenty-four years old, and she sat now in a barbecue restaurant on the Edenton waterfront. She wore dungarees that held onto the curve of her hips beautifully, and a stylish, tight-fitting embroidered Western shirt. She slowly ate her barbecue platter and frequently looked up at the sailboats and cabin cruisers as they passed the restaurant, headed for the docks at the end of Broad Street. She had stretched her dinner to an hour and a half as an impatient waitress waited for her departure.

To the waitress's frustration, and with several diners awaiting her table, Michelle ordered yet another beer. Shortly afterward, a forty-foot Sea Ray cabin cruiser slowly motored past. Michelle paid her bill without taking even a sip of her beer and went to her gold Cadillac Seville. It was ten years old, but it looked like new.

She drove three blocks down the street, parked at the docks, and watched through her heavily tinted windows as the captain and his mate secured the Sea Ray and walked past the Cadillac to a brand new Chevrolet truck. The skipper of the boat seemingly paid no attention to the woman in the Cadillac, but as he passed her car, he bent over to tie his shoe. There, he saw and retrieved an envelope tucked in the bumper.

At dark, Michelle boarded the vessel and entered the cabin. There were no smiles as she sat on the sofa with seven Pakistani men. Wearing dungarees and dirty white T-shirts, they smelled of four-days' travel without a shower. A private plane had flown them from Islamabad to Bermuda, where they had boarded a sport fishing boat that had taken them to the Oregon Inlet on the Outer Banks of North Carolina. There, they met up with the Sea Ray.

All were fluent in English, and listened intently as Michelle gave detailed instructions on the operation against Alpha Charlie. These men were all members of the Pakistani Army and had trained in intelligence operations with the British military. She gave them directions to the Swan Motel and keys to her Cadillac. They took five duffel bags stuffed with clothing and power tools.

Help had arrived.

As they drove away, Michelle started the engines of the Sea Ray and began motoring east on the Albemarle Sound, headed for Elizabeth City. She docked the boat there and walked in the dark to the nearby municipal airport.

There were no visible cars or people. At the far end of the small airfield, there stood a single Cessna, parked and unlocked.

More help.

Michelle opened the door of the Cessna, removed the keys from the ignition, and unlocked the luggage compartment. Everyone had followed her instructions. Inside the airplane lay thirty M-16 rifles, ten M-79 grenade launchers, and a crate filled with ammo and grenades. Nicole had told her they would need some serious hardware to kill the rogue drone operator, Alpha Charlie, and launch her missiles into America's heartland.

Home of Dr. Scott James
Jackson City, North Carolina
6:01 p.m.

I had to stop by my house. I needed some food, a shower, and maybe a few minutes to rest. Turning onto my block, I immediately saw red lights flashing everywhere in the dark. There were two police cars parked out front of my home.

A cop, on foot, stopped me in the driveway, and then walked over to my door. "Dr. James, I think it would be best if you stayed somewhere else tonight."

I could see my son, Kenny, waving at me from the upstairs window. Alicia opened the door, with the chain still attached, and called out, "Scott, go away or I'll tell them I want you arrested."

I was surprised by her words. I yelled back, "At least, tell me why you're doing this?"

"Just ... go. And read the morning paper. You'll see."

Alicia's best friend, Harriet, had a husband, John Graves, who was a reporter. Apparently someone fed him a front page story: "Plastic Surgeon Kills to Hide Office Love Affair."

Best Western Motel
Jackson City, North Carolina
7:14 p.m.

Alicia wouldn't even let me see the kids. I was in bad shape. I suddenly needed a place to stay. I had friends in town, but didn't want to be a bother. I went to the Best Western Motel and tried to pay with my Master Card. The clerk swiped the card several times and stood holding the credit card and looking at me.

I felt weird. At last, I asked, "Is there a problem?"

The man put his finger in his collar and moved it under his tie. Finally he responded. "Do you have another card? This one's declined."

I removed a second card, then a third, then a fourth.

Alicia had shut down all the accounts. I had a little money stashed at the office. I said to the motel clerk, "Save me a room. I'll be back in thirty minutes with cash."

9

Scott James Surgery Center
Jackson City, North Carolina
8:00 p.m.

 I PARKED MY CAR and ducked under the yellow police tape that surrounded the entire building. A smiling police officer greeted me right as I opened the front door.

"Hello, Doc. Remember me?"

I looked at the young policeman. He was short, African-American, and had a baby face. I shook my head. "You look familiar, but I'm sorry, I don't recall ... I'm not good with names."

"I'm Willie Wilson. You took care of my boy, Terrance. His brother hit him in the face when they were playing football together and cut his lip pretty bad. Broke his cheek bones, too. You fixed 'em and sewed him up about two years ago."

Although I still didn't remember the case, I smiled. "Does he have much of a scar?"

"Nope. You did a good job. And you never charged us a penny. That was cool of you. I never forgot that."

"Well, I'm glad I was able to help," I said as I started down the hall. As I opened the door to my office, Willie said, "Get lawyered up, Doc. From what I hear, you're in for a shit storm."

I spent time looking at my prize-winning orchids, and I thought about my life. Most of all, I missed my kids. I really wanted to see them but it seemed like, at least for now, my wife wasn't going to let me back in my own home. And she wasn't even allowing me to talk to them on the phone. I wished I could do something to help them get through what was going to be a rough time.

All I could do now was focus on what was at hand. I might be going to jail for a crime I didn't commit. I was confused and overwhelmed by it all.

Suddenly I was awakened from my thoughts by a deafening noise. *What was that?* I bounded from my office and ran to Willie. I could see him sitting in his chair at the end of the hall. "Is everything alright?" He didn't answer. I ran over to him, "Willie? Willie?"

He sat deathly still with his chair leaning back against the wall.

My heart thundered in my chest as I moved to him. Wilson's eyes were open and staring straight ahead. Blood trickled into his left eye and all the way down his neck, coming from a half-inch hole in the mid-forehead. Blood flowed from the back of his head, steadily feeding a growing pool around his chair. A gun lay on the floor beside him.

I touched Wilson's bloody neck and checked for a pulse. There was none.

A hallway door banged shut. Someone was running down the outside hall. I picked up the policeman's gun and ran from the office. The light was dim in the hall. I heard a shot and hit the floor. The assailant shot twice more at me and then took off. As I heard the door open, I jumped up and aimed Wilson's pistol at him. I pulled the trigger twice, but the gun didn't fire. I looked down to see that the magazine had been removed.

I ran out the door and watched as a black SUV spun its wheels on the pavement and roared onto Garden Avenue.

Within minutes, three police cars were there. Harris jumped from one as it rolled to a stop and yelled, "What the fuck were you thinking?" and then shook his head and stared at me.

I was covered in Wilson's blood. *Why did I pick up that stupid gun? And what was I thinking when I checked Wilson's bloody neck for a pulse? I knew damned well he was dead.*

I handed the police-issue pistol to him. Of course, my fingerprints were all over that gun. And unfortunately, it turned out that the gun was used to shoot Willie.

With his handkerchief, Harris took the weapon from me and handed it to one of the other officers. Harris then went to the side of the dead policeman and stood silently for a moment with his head bowed in reverence, as two white-suited EMTs watched. He knelt to inspect the head wound close up. Without saying a word, he gestured to another detective who handcuffed me.

I started yelling at Harris as they dragged me away to the police car. I knew that shouting would make me looking like a maniac, and I didn't care. "I didn't shoot Wilson! I was trying to get his assailant! Find the guy in the black SUV who was shooting at me! He's the one who killed Wilson!"

Harris signaled for the cop holding me to stop. "What'd he look like?"

In the excitement of the chase, I couldn't recall any distinguishing features. "I don't know. It was dark."

Harris shook his head and looked at me as if I were a little kid who just got caught shoplifting candy from a drugstore. "I imagine this is your supposed 'gigantic blond guy with a ponytail' again, right? C'mon, Doc, you can't expect me to believe that." Harris shook his head in disgust and turned to the other policemen. "Take the doctor."

"But—"

"Jesus Christ, Dr. James," Harris muttered.

10

NICOLE BANZAR SAT IN a class in the Marshall Taylor School of Drama. She had an interest in one of the students, Harold Simpkins. She had met him in Texas two months earlier and had encouraged him to enroll in drama school. She even paid his tuition. His instructor told her that after a full six weeks of acting school, Simpkins could still use more classes. That didn't matter to Nicole. It was time.

Nicole looked Simpkins over. About thirty years old, he was very thin, had sparse, sandy-colored hair, a soft chin, and a serious overbite. His unattractive appearance probably accounted for his failure to gain parts at the local community theaters.

When the class finally ended, Nicole told Simpkins she had something to talk to him about. She took him to a bar owned by a friend from Turkey and told him she was working for the government, and had an acting job for him. "There may be a terrorist cell operating on the eastern seaboard, with plans to bomb cities in America. We need you to help make their identity known."

He flatly refused, saying he wanted nothing to do with her employer, the CIA.

"Here, this is an advance payment," she said, laying $1,000 in front of him. "Take it, Harold. You need this."

He shook his head as she offered him the money.

"Nope. I need the money, but I ain't working for the CIA against no terrorists."

"But I haven't finished my offer. The CIA will give you ten thousand for helping this country. Your name will be in every newspaper in the country."

He looked at her, still shaking his head.

"And I'm attracted to strong heroic men like you. You're just the kind of guy I'd like to be my boyfriend."

That did it. Simpkins accepted the assignment and the money.

Jackson City Police Station
3:00 p.m.

None of the police departments were receptive. Harris simply looked wide-eyed at Simpkins, as if he wanted to laugh at him. "Appreciate ya comin' in, Agent Simpkins," Harris said to the man, putting emphasis on "*Agent*."

"It's imperative that we get full cooperation from the local police on this case," Simpkins said, "We're on the same team here, Detective. Any suspicious activities or evidence of foreign subversives, you call me immediately," he said, handing Harris a business card. *Foreign subversives? Agent? CIA?* The guy looked official enough, but his words seemed rehearsed. He was clearly nervous, too, and didn't have the cocky attitude Harris had come to expect from agents at the Federal level. Even the way he put out his hand to steady himself on the desk did not seem right.

Captain Mathew O'Brian, the police chief in Williamston, the municipality neighboring Jackson City, took Simpkins' card as he walked from the building. Simpkins started his rehearsed speech, but before he could say ten words, O'Brian emphatically stated, "There are no foreign nationals operating terrorist cells in the area, sir."

Simpkins further angered the police chief by placing his hand on O'Brian's shoulder while they walked. The police chief wiped the hand away and said, "Good day, sir."

The Swan Motel
Jackson City
7:06 p.m.

Simpkins returned after a day's work to a room at the Swan Motel, on the outskirts of Jackson City. In the room were five Pakistani men, all fluent in English. They wore T-shirts, wrinkled black trousers, and sandals. They smoked a heavy, dark tobacco, rolled in thick-veined, black tobacco leaves, ones that generated enough smoke to engulf the entire motel room in a thick cloud.

Simpkins tried not to think about who these men were. They didn't seem like CIA. But he had to admit it: The "acting" experience had been interesting. It put money in his pocket, *and* ... got him a date with Nicole tonight.

Simpkins told his Pakistani minders of his successful day. He was proud of the fact that not one of the people he had talked to during the day had noticed his primary objective—planting miniature microphones in the offices he visited. He'd managed to photograph most of the places he'd been to, as well. Simpkins had a hidden camera in his neck tie that was activated simply by touching the tie. Posing, vaguely, as a diligent Federal officer, he'd successfully photographed and bugged most of Jackson City's important buildings.

Three of the Pakistani men lay stretched out on the double bed and listened to Simpkins' tale. At the end, one commented to Simpkins that he'd done a good job and that he was free to go meet Nicole for his date now.

The Pakistani agents said nothing to Simpkins about it, but they were especially thrilled with the bug Simpkins positioned in one of the embroidered gold stars on the shoulder of Captain O'Brian's coat. If someone alerted the police to their presence, they'd probably know.

If they were lucky, it all might lead to Alpha Charlie.

Simpkins traded the suit they had lent him for his own dungarees, Justin boots, and Hawaiian sport shirt. In the parking lot, he switched from the rented Chevy to his Honda motorcycle and drove away.

There was little traffic on the rural road that was a shortcut back to Chapel Hill, so Simpkins was aware of a dark SUV that followed at a distance. Suddenly, he saw the lights of the vehicle approaching rapidly. He accelerated the motorcycle to seventy miles an hour. The SUV was doing ninety.

Simpkins moved to the far right of his lane to allow it to go by. The SUV slowed as it started to pass the bike. A man in the back seat stuck his head and shoulders out of the truck window and slammed the back of Harold Simpkins' neck with a baseball bat, just as a second, smaller man in the front seat leaned out his window and grabbed the motorcycle's handle bars. Simpkins went flying through the air, his body smashing against a tree.

The SUV braked. Simpkins was retrieved and wrapped in a tarp. The body and the motorcycle were thrown in the back of the SUV.

It was a professional job.

11

Jackson City Jail
Jackson City, North Carolina
11:00 a.m.

 AT MY ARRAIGNMENT, I was charged with first degree murder of Wilson and Dr. Carey, and the attempted murder of Elizabeth Keyes. My whole body shook. Harris stated, at the proceeding, "There's no proof that anyone other than Dr. James had been in the office at the time of the two deaths, and he was in the recovery room when the attempt to kill Keyes was made."

Bail was set at two million dollars. There was no way I could come up with that much money, especially after Alicia confiscated all of our bank accounts and then took the maximum cash possible out of all our credit cards and then canceled them. Alicia was a survivor and she was always good at taking care of herself.

Innocent or guilty, it looked like I was going away for a long time.

The Missile Game

I was led to a row of twelve jail cells. Each was designed to hold two inmates. All the men in this area were violent criminals, incarcerated for drug-related killings, rape, and armed robbery. It was a rough-looking group of men. We all wore the same blue prison suits. I was placed with a Hispanic male, Hector Mendez. He was an inch shorter than me, but must have been a hundred pounds heavier, although it was mostly fat. "Morning," I said, as I tried to sit down on my bed.

Mendez stood in my way and grunted, "Fuck you, white boy."

"And I was thinking we could be friends." I shrugged and tried to move around him. The other inmates sensed something was up and looked at us.

Mendez pulled out a homemade shiv. "Now, what the fuck you gonna do?"

I tried to ignore him and stay calm. "I was hoping to catch up on my sleep."

Mendez went berserk. He raised the knife and jumped toward me. I kept my eyes on the knife and as Mendez stabbed at my chest, I grabbed his wrist, twisted it, and threw him against the wall. Mendez dropped the knife and swung his fist wildly.

I stepped aside and pounded his face with a left and then hit him in the stomach with a right. Mendez turned to face me but his body was swaying, and his eyes did not focus.

"Racial profiling is not politically correct," I said.

With that, Mendez threw a hay maker punch, which missed me by a foot.

The other inmates were cheering, "Kill him! Kill him!"

I lifted my fist to finish him off, but saw no need. I led the defenseless Mendez to his bed and pushed him down.

Two guards were watching. Neither filed an incident report. And after that, nobody bothered me.

Soon, a black cloud of depression fell on me.

12

Drone Control Center, "Alpha Charlie"
Jackson City, North Carolina
12:05 p.m.

 CHARLIE SAT IN THE dark room and monitored the computer screens attached to the BAMS/UAS workstation. He wore special glasses that compensated for the low light conditions and which provided magnification, allowing him to view the text messages on the lower part of the screens. The BAMS/UAS portable control module used twenty hard drives, stacked one on top of the other and conveniently bolted to the left side of a flimsy-looking desk. The three monitors were each twenty inches wide and positioned at eye level to the operator. Active monitors came on when images were presented to them; blank monitors had no incoming videos.

Currently, the active screen pictured aerial views of a mountainous landscape. An hour earlier, Colonel Edwards had launched a Global Hawk RQ-4B, the newest and largest of the drone aircraft, from Kandahar, Afghanistan, and had placed a test target in an empty field a few miles from the base.

Edwards came on Charlie's headset and suggested a trial of the new chair. He told Charlie to be on the lookout for a fake truck, sitting on the test-firing range.

Charlie did as Edwards instructed, manipulating his new system to visualize the test area. He was pleased that he could move the aircraft easily. He could see the objective at five miles and elected to shoot at that distance. Each of his index fingers activated an X that moved and centered on the image. Pressing his right thumb on the red firing button, a Hellfire missile shot from the drone. After a delay of a few seconds, it struck the bull's eye painted on a cardboard replica of a truck and exploded on impact.

"Bra—*vo*," Edwards said.

REUTERS
Canberra, AUSTRALIA

The American Ambassador to Australia, Mr. David Martin, has been summoned back to Washington amid growing anger in the capital, Canberra, over allegations that the target of last week's foiled terrorist attack was a CIA-sponsored "black site" for the control of military drones in the Middle East. U.S. Officials, citing national security interests, have declined to comment on rumors that the three men and one woman apprehended last week in Sydney were actively searching for a drone control station rumored to be located somewhere in the vicinity of Byron Bay, a small resort town on the east coast of Australia. Members of the Australian Parliament on both the right and the left are calling for a full investigation of all civilian defense contractors doing business with the United States.

13

Chapel Hill, North Carolina
7:00 p.m.

FOUR YEARS AGO, BILLY Watson inherited the family peanut farm and a modest bank account. His low crop yield reflected his hatred of farming, and within two years, he was on the verge of bankruptcy. His friends and farm hands left him to a life of solitude. Each evening he went to the Varsity Bar, drank, and hit on women. All of Chapel Hill knew he was a drunkard and a drug addict, so none of the girls showed any interest in him. But he didn't care.

Tonight, things were different. A new girl from out of town seemed interested. She was young and pretty. Her eyes were brown and her long blonde hair curled up as it touched her shoulders. Her face was smooth and pear-shaped, with prominent cheekbones. She didn't seem to mind that his rough beard hadn't been trimmed in six months, his unkempt hair hadn't been combed in weeks, and his eyes were so blood shot from inebriation that their color was in question. Billy couldn't keep his eyes off her large breasts.

Michelle drank wine as he ordered Vodka, straight up. "I'm from Suthern Jaw-ja," she said in a made-up accent that even the inebriated farmer knew was false.

"So, tell me, really, are you from New York or is it Jersey?"

She blushed, "Am I that bad as a southern belle?"

"Yeah, well no. As the southern belle, you're prettier'n any girls from the South I've ever met, but you talk like a Yankee trying to imitate Scarlett O'Hara. Better stick to 'Naw-thun' talk."

As they laughed she moved close to him. "You're cute," she said as one of her breasts rested on his arm.

Soon, sex was the only thing on his mind. She was willing and wanted to go back to his farm house. He drove his pickup as she followed in a gold Cadillac Seville.

At the farm, an excited Billy Watson jumped out of his vehicle and ran to hers. As he helped her from the Cadillac, she rubbed his crotch and pulled his head to her chest. His virility had suffered from the alcohol and coke, but it was back tonight. She undressed in his bedroom, and then he watched as she crawled, naked, onto the bed, and then on top of him.

Suddenly four men and a tall brunette walked into the room and stood by his bed. He sat up abruptly, "What the ...?"

Nicole shoved him back down. Each man grabbed an extremity.

Billy struggled, kicking and screaming. "Michelle! Do you know these people?"

Michelle reached over and pinched his cheek firmly and leaned her face to within a few inches of his. "Billy, I need your fuckin' farm and I don't need you to plant fuckin' *peanuts* on it."

Billy started to weep. "Please, I'll do whatever."

"You're fuckin' pathetic. Where's my knife, Nicole?" Michelle asked.

"Don't hurt me."

Nicole handed her a hunting knife with an eight-inch blade.

Michelle ran it down his neck. "Nobody screws me without paying." She laid the blade of the knife against his windpipe. She pressed the knife until blood oozed from a shallow cut. Billy pulled against the men restraining him.

"You're what's wrong with America," she screamed. "The free ride is over!"

She grabbed his penis. With a single swipe of the blade, she cut it off. Billy screamed in agony. She shoved the organ down his throat, choking him.

He mustered all his strength to pull away, but the four men held him down firmly. Michelle pressed a pillow over his face until his struggling ceased.

14

Kandahar, Afghanistan
9:30 a.m.

MAJOR GENERAL AHMAD KAHN of the Afghanistan National Air Force flew by helicopter from his headquarters in Kabul to the airfield adjoining the American drone hangars on the outskirts of the city. The hangars were isolated on the perimeter of the Afghani Air Force facility, which was home base for Russian-made Mi-15 and Mi-24 helicopters, as well as Russian Antonov cargo transports.

One of Kahn's spies had told him the drones were being moved to a base in Iraq. After the copter landed, a waiting jeep took Kahn to the American commanding the drone operation, Colonel Edwards. Without a word of greeting, the two men shook hands coldly.

Kahn was abrupt in stating the purpose of his visit. "I forbid you from moving your drones without my permission!"

"The first time I reported to your fuckin' office about

bringing two of our drones, the Predators, to Kandahar, the Taliban put a fuckin' IED in the hangar we were assigned to," Edwards said. "It killed two of my men."

"I don't care. I order you to keep the drones here!"

"Well, old buddy, the rules have changed," Edwards said, putting his hands on his hips. "I'm not moving them back."

"But the leaks have been sealed. There are no more spies in my office."

"Bullshit!" Edwards snapped. He then turned on his heel and walked away.

On his way back to the helicopter, Kahn sent a text message to Kahlil in Damascus.

Damascus, Syria
3:05 p.m.

For 150 years, Ambuda Kahlil's family had been making and selling oriental rugs near the Bab Tuma (St. Thomas's Gate) in the old, walled city of Damascus. Kahlil had followed in his father's footsteps. With his good eye for selecting and weaving the highest quality rugs, his business had expanded, as had his bank account. Recently his friends in ISIS had convinced him to become an important financial contributor, and along with sending a cash donation, he'd also begun using his business to secretly relay messages between ISIS allies.

Kahlil felt the Blackberry in his pocket vibrate. The incoming text read: AMERICAN DRONE BASE LEAVING KANDAHAR. MY CONTACT SAYS MOVING TO IRAQ

Upon receipt of the message in Damascus, Kahlil forwarded it to a courier for delivery to Jorad Hormand.

15

Jackson City Hospital
1:15 p.m.

 THE BATTERY OF NEW tests ordered for Elizabeth Keyes was extensive. Her Valium level dropped precipitously, but her deep sleep continued. By the next day, she was somnolent but responsive. Detective Harris paid a visit to her bedside.

"Missus Keyes," he asked, "do ya have any old boyfriends, a husband in your past, or any people that threatened or wanted to hurt ya?"

"No. All my relationships have ended cordially."

"Do ya have anything ya want ta tell me? Like about you and Dr. James?"

"What about us?"

"The *Chronicle* says you two were lovers."

She lifted her head and gave a weak laugh. "That's a crock. Some reporter with a vivid imagination must have written that. Dr. James is a straight arrow. That guy only has eyes for his beauty queen wife. Everybody knows that."

Jackson City Police Station
Jackson City, North Carolina
2:30 p.m.

Harris had taken a half a dozen calls from the Mayor and City Council members, all asking about the murders. He was taking a swig of coffee when the phone rang yet again. It was Herb Waters, the top dog at Jackson City Hospital.

"James is guilty as hell. Do not let him out of jail!" Waters barked.

Harris said he was busy and hung up the phone.

Harris fiddled with the cords of his string tie while he sifted through one of the filing cabinets confiscated from James' office. As he'd expected, he was coming up empty — just folder after folder filled with charts and photos of happy patients hugging Dr. James.

Harris drank his coffee and paced around the office before returning to the files that James kept. He was intrigued by a file labeled "Jackson City Hospital." Inside was a newspaper obituary of Cabot Barnes, a Jackson City Hospital board member from 1997 until his death in July 1999. Harris read the obit, as well as a news clipping that pictured the forty-year-old computer programmer/entrepreneur, and reported his death by drowning at sea, thirty-five miles off the Oregon Inlet. Barnes had been with six buddies at the time, aboard his fifty-five-foot Viking sport-fishing boat.

Barnes was a local hero. He'd been the captain of the high school swim team. He'd led Jackson City to a championship his senior year, then received a full scholarship to a state college. Barnes married his high school sweetheart, was a father of two children, and became the favorite coach of the local youth soccer teams.

Harris suddenly stopped reading. *A champion swimmer drowns near a boat with six other men aboard and a stock of life preservers and throwing buoys?*

Another folder contained brief notes about another Jackson City Hospital board member, Quinton Jolly, who'd died a few days after Barnes. Jolly was found in a hospital call room with a plastic bag wrapped over his face. The coroner had ruled it a suicide.

Harris shivered.

Most of the documents in the file related to a lengthy article Dr. James had written and sent to the *Daily Chronicle*, where it was published in the "Letters to the Editor" section. The article referred to the alleged pending sale of the non-profit Jackson City Hospital to AHS, a large conglomerate of for-profit hospitals. James pointed out that hospital costs would increase even higher than they already had, resulting in the reduction or elimination of charitable care. Of even more significance, Jackson City Hospital had in escrow over two hundred million dollars from its profitable ventures. James raised the question of where all that money would go if the hospital were to be sold.

James had done his research and even quoted sections of the hospital's original charter. James contended that selling a hospital with a longstanding charter as a nonprofit facility to a for-profit group would be a violation of its charter. James emphatically stated that the city could rightfully claim ownership of the hospital. The money used to start up the hospital in 1931, and to build the new hospital in 1975, had come from fundraisers and city appropriations. This bound the hospital to ownership by the community.

Harris went through the minutes of the hospital board's actions, starting in 1995. James had circled sections of the minutes in red ink and had made extensive notations. Over a fifteen-year period, the original charter of the hospital was amended several times. On November 10, 1999, the hospital bylaws were amended to specify that the hospital's chief executive officer was solely responsible for appointing the hospital's Board of Directors. James had made a note on the margin: "The Board appoints the hospital's Chief Executive? A Board appointed by that *same* Chief Executive?"

Scratching his chin, Harris wondered how many people knew of this flip-flop in the appointments of the directors and the chief administrator. His question was answered, at least in part, when he read the minutes of a 1999 hospital board meeting, minutes that James had circled in red: "Cabot Barnes and Quinton Jolly questioned the circular appointments of the board members and administrators."

<u>16</u>

Near the Iraqi-Kurdistan Border
12:08 p.m.

TWO OBSERVERS HID IN a mountain ridge a quarter-mile from the drone hangar, where six American drones had been delivered in covered trucks a week before. Although the observers wore military boots, they were dressed in traditional Arab garb.

Over the previous days, from their hide-out, the two Iraqis had caught glimpses of men in American Air Force uniforms assembling drones—four MQ-9 Reapers and two RQ-4A Global Hawks. The Reaper weighed nearly two tons and the Global Hawk twelve tons. They carried payloads of 3,800 pounds, more than triple the load carried by the previous generation of drone, the Predator.

Now, inside the hangar, American crews loaded Hellfire and Sidewinder missiles onto all the drone aircraft, while on the ridge one of the observers sent a message.

Damascus, Syria
12:19 p.m.

Kahlil felt the Blackberry in his pocket vibrate. Excusing himself from an Australian couple shopping for an antique Tabriz rug in his shop, he went to the back room and read the message: AIRCRAFT ASSEMBLED AND READY FOR COMBAT.

Kahlil slipped into a closet and uncovered his radio equipment. He sent a coded message: MY INFORMANT SAYS YOUR AMERICAN IS PREPARING DRONES. TARGET MUST BE ISIS.

Washington, DC
9:00 p.m.

Omar Farok read a text message on his cell phone: ARIANA TO HORMAND: PRODUCT NEAR COMPLETION. NEED GUIDANCE SYSTEMS. $1 MILLION EACH. PLEASE MAKE DEPOSIT.

Farok was a filthy rich thirty-five-year-old prince from the Sudan who traveled around the world, sponsoring terrorism. Small and thin, he had a finely featured, clean-shaven face, framed with black hair, large almond-shaped brown eyes, and ribbon-like lips that barely moved when he spoke, which was always in a soft, silky voice. Farok owned a fleet of Learjets that carried him to whatever country would allow him to enter. Although he'd been suspected and even accused of terrorism, there had never been sufficient evidence to prosecute.

A year earlier, the United States had managed to ban his entry into the country on a technicality. But that was purely a formality for a man of his means. Now, here he was—in the nation's capitol. If he got caught, he'd be deported or detained. He'd have to be clever and stealthy. *Not so much*, he thought, sniffing arrogantly as the corners of his mouth curled up in a stiff smile. *So stupid, these Americans*.

Watson Farm
Chapel Hill, North Carolina
Noon

Sandra had become one of twelve "soldiers" when Nicole Banzar had recruited her from the Chicago Al Qaeda splinter group. She was an attractive twenty-one-year-old with long, wavy, bleach-blonde hair. Her assignment for the three days prior to the killing of the farm owner, Billy Watson, was to hide in the woods nearby and simply observe. Nicole wanted to be certain her soldiers would not be burdened by Billy's friends or curious neighbors.

During the observation period, no one turned into the driveway, and only six cars, other than the daily passing of the mailman, even drove past the property. This was what Nicole wanted—total isolation to do her work. Billy

Watson's farm was the perfect setting.

Sandra, like the rest of Nicole's soldiers, was now dressed as a farmer. She was sitting on a tractor beside the road when a beat-up Chevy Camaro pulled into the dirt driveway. Sandra started the Ford 8N tractor and drove to block the passage of the visitor.

"Can I help ya?" she called out to the driver.

The man was rough-looking: unshaven, homemade tattoos covering the visible parts of his skin, dressed in a dirty T-shirt and grease-smudged jeans. He looked Sandra over, top to bottom, and focused on her breasts as he spoke. "Naw, ya cain't help me. I'm Earl. Jes goin' ta see Billy. Sometimes he needs a little help 'round here, an' I need a little money for a carb'rator, so's I'll jes run on down." Racing his engine, he drove around Sandra into the weed-overgrown field and sped to the house. He screeched to a stop, bounded out of the car, and strode up to the front door.

Nicole stepped outside and closed the door after her. "Billy's sick. He ain't seein' visitors today."

"I don't want to talk ta you. I jes wanna see Billy."

Pushing her aside, he opened the door and walked into the room—where a guy dressed like a farmer and carrying an M-16 immediately greeted him. The fake farmer aimed the rifle at Earl's chest. Wide-eyed, Billy's buddy raised his hands high over his head. Sweat broke out all over him.

"I don't mean no harm," he said. "Where's Billy? Tell

him Earl's here. I jes need ta say sumthin' ta him."

Nicole rushed in behind Earl. "Don't shoot!"

The soldier lowered his gun to his waist but kept it pointed at the man. "Hands behind your back," Nicole barked.

She duct-taped his wrists and then his thighs and knees together.

Earl began to cry. "What'cha doin' ta me? I don't have nuthin' 'gainst ya'll. I jus' wanna see Billy!"

"You don't always get what you want," she said as she rolled out a large sheet of clear, heavy-duty plastic and shoved him onto it. While the male soldier held Earl down, Nicole folded the plastic neatly around him and taped all the open edges, making it airtight.

Earl kicked and screamed inside his sealed pouch. "Please let me go! I'll jes go an' say nothin' 'bout all this. Please don't kill me!" His voice was muffled by the plastic wrap. The more he struggled and cried, the faster his oxygen was being used up. His voice grew weaker and weaker until he went silent, suffocated in his plastic cocoon.

Nicole turned to the soldier. "Stick him in a closet till midnight, then put him in his car and drive it into the Roanoke River outside Weldon. Make sure there's no tape residue on his body or clothing, and don't leave any fingerprints. Pour booze down his throat and make this look like a car accident."

17

Kirkuk, Iraq
1:00 p.m.

COLONEL EDWARDS HAD JUST received an urgent call. A Kurdish spy near Mosul had spotted a convoy of deuce-and-a-half trucks carrying forty ISIS troops. Shar al Sheikh was in the group. Charlie's Global Hawk was still airborne and within ten miles of the target.

"Damn, they're bold!" Edwards said. "They think Charlie's still setting up his station in America and isn't operational yet. They feel safe, and traveling in the open saves them a lot of time."

As the drone closed in on the convoy, one of the forensics team watching the monitors stood and shouted, "There it is! What in the hell are they doing, exposing themselves like that? They know we're looking for 'em!"

Charlie was already in his control center when an excited Edwards called.

"Charlie! We have ducks on the pond! Four of 'em, all

in a row."

"What's the bounty?"

"On Shar al Sheikh, twenty million. But for a convoy, I'll authorize another twenty, but only if you kill most of 'em."

Charlie flopped into his chair and activated the monitors. Screen A showed the convoy of four trucks on level terrain and out in the open. Screen B showed a close-up of the leader, sitting by the driver in the lead truck. The headcount was ten per vehicle.

"Is the identity of al Sheikh confirmed?"

"Yes, sir. His photos are exact matches for the Shar al Sheikh who helped plan 9-11. He's all yours. There are four Hellfires in the tubes. Blast those motherfuckers to hell."

Charlie got down to business. His heart beat fast and sweat dripped from his brow. He quickly placed the square on the front truck and centered the X. He wanted to kill all four, but there was one problem: The trucks were spaced fifty feet apart. The cloud of dust from the first missile explosion would obscure his view of the rest of the targets. The men could leave the trucks and disappear before he fired his second shot. He moved the sight back and forth along the path of the trucks and measured the distance between them.

"I'm going for a hat trick plus one," Alpha Charlie said aloud to the forensics crew in Iraq.

He pushed the trigger button on the first truck and in

rapid-fire succession fired the other three Hellfires as he moved the sights along the path of the road.

His forensics team all stood silent, holding their breath. None of the group, including Edwards, had ever seen this done before, and Charlie had done it only in video games. The first explosion would be in ten seconds. Charlie counted to himself: *ten, nine, eight, seven, six ...*

When his count reached zero, a cloud of dust smothered the convoy. In the ensuing three seconds, the dust cloud enlarged in a long, linear path. Charlie's fists clenched as he waited. Twenty-five seconds elapsed before he was able to see through the dust cloud. There were the four trucks, all bombed out.

A cheer arose from his crew in Iraq. Charlie half-smiled and gave a salute.

18

Jackson City Jail
Midnight

I SAT ALONE IN my jail cell, staring at the wall as if in a trance, thinking about my wife. A bitter chuckle rose in my throat, like bile, at the irony of it all. The thing that had attracted her to me had now turned out to be the same thing that drove her away. I was a plastic surgery resident at Duke when Alicia's mother was mugged and beaten. Her facial bones were shattered and I stayed at her side for four days and nights until the tracheotomy tube was removed and she could breathe on her own.

Though Alicia was courted by wealthy and successful men, she fell in love with me because I was the one who stayed at her mother's side the whole time. Of course, that was long ago, at a time when small-town doctors actually cared about helping people. Things had changed. Healthcare costs were through the roof, and they were only going to go higher with the sale of the non-profit Jackson City Hospital.

Alicia had initially loved me for being so dedicated to my patients, but then over the years, she grew to hate that very same quality.

From jail, I called our family lawyer. After he told me that he had filed papers to prevent me from seeing my two boys and that he was representing my wife in the divorce, he hung up on me. I thought that was very sweet of him. I then called three other lawyers whom I considered to be close friends. They all refused to represent me when they found out that all my assets were frozen and I had no money for a retainer.

Sure, the test for nitrates on my hands was negative, proving that I didn't fire the gun that killed Wilson—but what good did that do me? Everything else pointed to murder. I'd been at the scene of two killings and an attempt on Keyes' life in less than forty-eight hours. The judge and prosecutor didn't care about the nitrate test.

For the first time in my life, I was ready to give up. My head was spinning. *What the hell am I going to do?* I was so filled with anxiety I couldn't think straight. I couldn't think at all. I just sat there, dumbstruck and seriously depressed. I was used to adversity, but nothing could've prepared me for the troubles confronting me now. I was raised on a tobacco farm and for years worked long into the night doing farming chores to help my aged parents barely eke out a living. My muscles grew strong from the farm work and this helped make me a good athlete. On the high school football team, Herb Waters and I were in the backfield together. Herb was fullback and I was tailback. I was offered a football scholarship but instead chose an academic scholarship at a state college. During the summers, I worked on the farm, and during the academic year I took on a few campus jobs to make extra money for my parents. There was no time for sports. I made high grades in college and med school, and excelled in my surgical training.

I'd trained for surgery under Dr. Jerome Fusco. Under his regime I had to be prepared at any time to quote articles from the thirty or so surgical journals published each month. I had to study and memorize the techniques of each operation in which I was involved, so that if a surgeon on the case fell ill, I could take over. At the same time, I had to provide patient care during killer shifts of "on thirty-six, off twelve" hours. After my paperwork was finished, that often meant zero off hours.

Now all those years of hard work and training seemed to be for naught. I lay on my bed that night thinking about what to do next, but the mental and physical toughness that I'd developed in the tobacco fields was gone. I wished I had the $1.5 million I spent building my surgery center for facial reconstruction. With no surgery on the books, there was no income coming in. I was screwed. I was broke and there was no way I was ever going to make bail. All the extra work I had put into my surgical training seemed like a thing of the past now.

Earlier in the day, one of the guards had read aloud a brief article to me and my jail mates. It told of Herb Waters, who was now the president of Jackson City Hospital, being seen in town having dinner with my wife. My knees grew weak. My chest ached. If I had Wilson's gun again, this time I'd shoot *myself*.

19

Watson Farm
Chapel Hill, North Carolina
9:06 a.m.

 THE TOP OF THE Mack's trailer had been peeled back, and the terrorist recruits were assembling the launchers on the truck bed. The four men and two women were dressed as farmers. Nearby, the chief engine mechanic had been working on the deceased Billy Watson's backhoe for two hours. Ideally, the old vehicle would be used to move the missiles quickly, from the crates to the launchers.

But the old diesel engine just wouldn't turn over. The chief mechanic wiped sweat from his face with his forearm, smearing grease on his face, and muttered, "Can't get the son-of-a-bitch started."

Michelle came into the barn and walked over to fix the truck herself. "I need that machine. Get the fuck outta my way."

As she approached the vehicle, the mechanic stepped

toward her, and as she bent down to take a look, he copped a feel of her ass. Michelle laughed, shrugged, and then hit him in the jaw, knocking him to on the ground. She scowled, "I'll cut off your balls and shove 'em up your ass if you even think of touchin' me again."

The man held his jaw and apologized. "God, Michelle, I didn't mean anything by it."

Michelle kicked him in the side with the pointed toe of her Western boot, and screamed, "Don't fucking touch me!"

One of the other men pulled her away before she killed him. Michelle took the mechanic's tools and began working on the old diesel engine. Within thirty minutes, she had the engine running.

Michelle had trained in Israel with some of the best weapons experts in the world. She'd worked with missiles confiscated by the border police as well as Scud missiles that had been fired their way but had fallen short. She'd learned how to take the devices apart, piece by piece, and repurpose them. She'd removed the kerosene-propelled motors and converted them to solid fuel engines. She'd added GPS guidance systems to relics of past wars and had made them capable of hitting targets 200 miles away.

Now, Michelle headed up the covert operation in the United States, where, among other things, she was charged with installing automatic target recognition (ATR) guidance systems in the silkworms. Manufactured by General

Electric, the ATRs had been legally sold to Israel for the development of its missile defense system. Using money Hormand had sent, Nicole had purchased six of these units at black-market prices from Michelle's Israeli "friends."

Michelle had worked through the night trying to get all six missiles ready. In the summer heat, she sweated profusely. Since she never wore a bra, her nipples were visible through her wet blouse, yet no one in the group dared to glance at her chest. Although most of the men were devout Muslims, none objected to Michelle's revealing attire.

Michelle was in the process of installing the ATRs when she received a package from Hormand containing an attachment developed for naval warfare. In mid flight, the attachment could locate the GPS signal given out by a ship in trouble, and accurately lock on to the distressed vessel. Hormand had sent only one of these devices, which Michelle was to install in the first rocket that would be fired.

When she finally finished, she announced, "The missiles are ready. They're accurate enough to hit the United States Capitol from here—if that was our target—and they would be powerful enough to flatten the motherfucker! As soon as Celena gets off her ass and locates the real target, our missiles are going to rip this country open."

Cambridge, Maryland
9:15 p.m.

At long last, the ISIS chief could send a text to Kahlil: MY MISSILES ARE READY TO STRIKE. AFTER CHARLIE IS DEAD, I WILL AUTHORIZE THE USE OF ALL MY MISSILES TO DESTROY THE CITY. PRAISE ALLAH.

Jackson City, North Carolina
11:30 p.m.

Celena, Hormand's operative, checked her texts. THE AMERICAN AND HIS CONTROL STATION MUST BE LOCATED AND DESTROYED BEFORE HE KILLS MORE OF MY ISIS BROTHERS. DEADLINE IS ONE WEEK.

20

Jackson City Police Station
11:00 a.m.

 HARRIS WAS STUMPED, AND worried. Someone had paid James' full bail with cash, and it wasn't a bail bondsman. After more than twenty telephone calls, Harris still hadn't identified James' mysterious benefactor. Judge Wilkins refused to give him the name, and nobody at the courthouse seemed to know where the money had come from.

Harris tightened his jaw. *Not gonna do it. Not til I have ta.*

Harris figured that ignoring the release order might at least buy him some time to track down who was behind this, and it would keep the hospital president, Herb Waters, off his back.

It wasn't time enough. After making a few phone calls that led nowhere, Harris was nosing around on the computer when a courier delivered a memo from the judge: "RELEASE JAMES NOW OR I WILL CHARGE YOU

WITH CONTEMPT OF COURT."

A few seconds later, his phone rang. Judge Wilkins made no attempt to mask the annoyance in her voice. "Dr. James' bail has been paid. He's free to go. The court has sent his release orders. Make sure he understands that he cannot leave the city for any reason. Failure to comply with any of the terms of the release will result in his arrest and forfeiture of the two million in bail, every dollar of it. Tell Dr. James that if he cannot afford an attorney, call the public defender's office. I'll see him in court in September. I suggest you get moving."

A contempt charge came with a $10,000 fine and jail time. Harris dropped his head and shook it. *Shit*.

21

Jackson City Jail
1:25 p.m.

 HARRIS WALKED UP TO my jail cell and unlocked the door. He didn't say a word, didn't even look at me. I just stood inside the cage I'd been dying to get out of, staring at the open door. I tried to make eye contact with him and read his expression, but he wasn't giving anything up.

When I was released from jail, I had no plan, no car, and very little cash in my wallet. I decided to walk around town for a while, hoping to clear my mind and figure out what to do next. An hour later I was crossing Magnolia Avenue when I heard a woman's voice yell my name. Raising my forearm to shade my eyes from the sun's glare, I looked in the direction of the voice and saw an arm waving at me through the open window of an aging, fender-dented, white Honda Accord. As I approached the car, the driver called out again, "Dr. James!" It was Elizabeth Keyes.

.Elizabeth Keyes had been my office manager for the

past two months. Never before had a staff member endeared herself so quickly. Everyone who came in contact with Elizabeth liked her. It probably didn't hurt that the thirty-two-year-old blonde was fashion-model gorgeous.

"Elizabeth." I said, surprised to see her. "Good to see you. Clearly, you're feeling better than last time I saw you."

"Likewise."

"Thanks." I stood for a moment, then said, "Poor Boyd."

"Yeah. Dr. Carey. That's so sad."

Then, lowering her voice, she asked, "So you're a free man now?"

"Um, well, sort of … " I stammered. "At least for now. I'm out on bail."

"Wow! How'd you come up with all that money? The paper said it was, like, two million."

"I didn't," I said quietly. "Someone else paid it."

"Do you know who?"

I shook my head and looked around nervously. This was not a conversation to be having with an employee who also happened to be the patient who'd almost died in my operating room. After all, that unfortunate incident was being investigated as an attempted murder, for which I was the prime suspect.

Leaning toward the car's open window, I said, "Well, I'd better get going. I'm glad to see you're doing well. Take care, Elizabeth."

"Dr. James," Keyes called after me as I stepped away from the car. "Do you need a ride somewhere?"

I hesitated, not sure I wanted to trade the freedom of walking for the confines of a car. But then I thought, *Maybe Keyes knows something I don't, like what happened to the friend who was supposed to pick her up. Maybe she saw someone else in the OR . . .*

"Sure," I said.

As I got into the front passenger seat, I couldn't help but notice that her curves were accentuated by her skin-tight T-shirt and workout pants. "You look a lot better than the last time I saw you. But are you sure you're okay now?"

"All better!"

"You had me worried there," I said.

"Oh, I just had too much Valium. Once it wore off, I was fine," she said. "Where to, James? Your house or mine?"

This was a side of Keyes I'd never seen, and it caught me a little off-guard. But I liked it.

"Well, since my wife gave me the boot and started screwing around, I don't have a home to go to," I said. "But you can take me to a hotel."

"And you're going to pay for that how?" she asked.

How does she know I'm broke? Before I could ask the question, Keyes answered it. "Rumor has it your wife cleaned you out, and since you haven't been able to work … " Turning toward me, her face filled with empathy, she laid her hand on my leg and cooed, "I'm so sorry all this is happening to you. You're welcome to stay at my place."

"Alright."

"In separate bedrooms, of course," she added quickly.

My two options flashed through my mind: Sleep on a park bench, or go home with a beautiful woman. It took all of two seconds to decide.

"Are you sure?" I asked.

"Positive."

"It'll just be for a couple days, till I figure something else out."

"Buckle up, Doc," she said as she pulled the Accord away from the curb.

"Could we stop by my office on the way?"

"You're allowed in there?"

"I just want to check on my orchids."

"You and your orchids. Can they wait till tomorrow? I'm all sweaty from my Zumba class and really want to get home and shower. And I've got a ton of stuff to do today."

I had no choice but to agree.

22

Hangar 9
Camp Peary, Virginia
1:25 p.m.

CAMP PEARY SITS ON a 9,200-acre parcel of land separated from the rest of Virginia by an eight-foot chain-link fence topped with barbed wire. About 8,000 acres are wooded, and 2,000 cleared acres are used for military housing and training areas. The enormous, three-mile-long airstrip at the base is surrounded on one side by the York River and on the other by the 400-acre Bigler's Millpond.

The airfield at Camp Peary is the most technologically advanced runway in the U.S. defense system. It can accommodate the largest aircraft in the world. Embedded in the concrete are sensors that measure wind speed and direction, barometric pressure, air temperature, cloud and fog cover, and precipitation. At times of dangerous weather conditions in Washington D.C, planes flying important government officials to the capital are rerouted here.

Apart from such emergency situations, the Camp

Peary airstrip is closed to all civilian and military aircraft, and is reserved, with special clearance, for high-ranking military officers, and for secret landings by the world's most important diplomats. Though shrouded in secrecy, the camp has long been rumored to be a training base for the CIA, used for the testing of various classified materials and equipment.

In this isolated and secured environment, three men now worked under the body of an MQ-1 drone, or Predator, as it was known. The unmanned aircraft was small — only twenty-seven feet long, with a wingspan of forty-eight feet. For three days, the men had been fitting a direct energy laser system to the underbelly of the aircraft. The little pilotless airplane only stood about four and a half feet off the ground, and that made for back-breaking work.

Never before had a laser weapon system been installed on a drone aircraft. In the past, existing laser systems had been too heavy. Operational lasers, such as the type President Reagan had proposed in his Star Wars plan for missile defense, weighed over five tons.

The leader of the laser group, Jacob Weizman, was a thin, balding Israeli in his 60s. Generally, he gave instructions to the other two men, and then before they could perform each assignment, elbowed them away and did the work himself.

Alpha Charlie, wearing sunglasses, a Redskins cap, and a sweatshirt, watched at a distance. He smiled as he witnessed the interaction between the owner of the aircraft company and his men. Both of his guys had been with him for twenty or more years.

Weizman held a variety of patents on pilotless aircraft and weapon systems for drones. Over the past decade, Weizman's California-based company had successfully sold six different drone prototypes to the U.S. Air Force. For the past three years, his attention had been focused solely on direct energy laser systems.

It was Weizman who had sponsored the gaming competition that Charlie had won, and Weizman who had urged the CIA to recruit Charlie. And it was Charlie who in turn had the money to buy his own aircraft and finance Weizman's research. The CIA didn't have enough money assigned to drone operations to get the job done.

So it was that the CIA and Charlie became partners.

Charlie had started by financing his own fleet of four, MQ-1 Predators, the first and most commonly-used type of drone, all of which were now operational and combat tested. As Charlie's fees—and reputation—grew to legendary status, he had plans to buy more aircraft, including the Predator's successor, the MQ-9 Reaper, and eventually, the biggest one of them all, the RQ-4B Global Hawk.

At last, the old engineer stood back, folded his arms, and smiled. Weizman waved Charlie over to talk. Despite having resided in California for so long, Weizman still spoke with a strong Israeli accent. It was so bad at times that even the men who worked with him had a hard time understanding.

"They're still saying it can't be done. But this will show them." he said to Charlie. "The weight of this DE Laser is only 1,100 pounds. It's the same weight as the Hellfire system that MQ-1s now use."

Weizman's reduction in the poundage of electrical wiring needed to make all the connections, lighter metals in the casings, and the newest lithium batteries, had shaved a half-ton off the weight. His innovations allowed directed electromagnetic radiation to melt the wiring in ground vehicles, and more importantly, the guidance and detonation systems of modern missiles. He felt the laser could even destroy the wiring systems in ships.

Hitting stationary or slow-moving trucks or cars would be of course easy, but achieving Weizman's dream, hitting and destroying missiles in flight, would be tough, very tough.

"No one has ever used the DE system to arm drones, but with this small unit, I will do it. With your skills, Charlie, we'll make history," Weizman said.

Charlie slapped the thick lenses on the laser pod. "I'm looking forward to testing these babies."

23

Keyes' Apartment
Jackson City, North Carolina
3:30 p.m.

 KEYES PARKED THE ACCORD in the carport of a two-story fourplex in need of refurbishing. The inside of her second-floor apartment was equally outdated.

"Please, sit down and relax while I take a quick shower," she said as we walked in. "Then I'll make us something to eat."

Half an hour later I was standing at the sink, hand-washing the dishes, when suddenly Elizabeth appeared by my side, startling me. She stood so close I could feel her breath. She smelled wonderful ... like a white orchid.

"Your turn," she said, holding out a fresh washcloth and bath towel. "Go take a nice, hot shower while I throw dinner together."

It was an offer I couldn't refuse. The showers at the jail were short and lukewarm. The food was disgusting, and I hadn't eaten anything since breakfast: two rubbery eggs, burnt toast, greasy fried potatoes, and watery orange juice. After being released, I'd been tempted to get lunch at a café downtown but decided against spending any of the little money I had.

I was famished.

"You know, that sounds really good."

Keyes' Apartment
5:20 pm

I walked into the dining room to find Elizabeth carrying two plates of spaghetti and meatballs from the kitchen. Already on the table were a bottle of red wine, a bowl of green salad, and place settings for two. After choking down jail grub, that simple meal was looking good to me.

"Just in time," she said, smiling. "That was one long shower. I was starting to worry about you in there."

"Aren't you worried about being alone with an accused killer?"

"Nah. I trust you."

"Well, you're the only one who does," I said. "And the way the investigation is going—" I stopped myself from saying more.

"You can tell me all about it over dinner," Keyes said.

"And spoil a perfectly good meal talking about my

hideous problems? Let's just enjoy dinner now." Then, lifting my wine glass, I toasted, "Bon appétit!"

While we ate the satisfying meal and drank the cheap wine, we made small talk. Every few minutes, Keyes would slip in a question about my case, and I'd sidestep the question or answer it cryptically, then change the subject. As dinner wore on, my discomfort increased. Just being there seemed surreal. I mean, I barely even *knew* this woman.

The only time I'd previously spent with Keyes was at work, and our relationship was always all business. We rarely spoke, and our communication was limited to matters relating to patients and running the office.

There was virtually no personal information on her job application; she'd even left the space for emergency contacts blank. She didn't wear a wedding ring, and had no personal photos on her desk. She never talked about her family, either, so I had no idea whether she had a husband or boyfriend, or children, or siblings. The only mention of a friend had been the name of the no-show, Anna Duke, who was supposed to have transported her home the day of surgery.

I knew from her job application that she'd graduated from a nursing school in Texas, but I didn't know if she'd been born and raised there or moved there from somewhere else. When I was opening the surgery center, I'd been so busy that I'd hired Keyes without checking references and after only a ten-minute phone interview.

During the two months she'd worked for me, prior to Dr. Carey's murder, she had done an excellent job and was always cordial to me and the rest of the staff. But she'd never formed a personal connection with or socialized outside the office with any of us. Now, here I was in her apartment ...

Who is she?

Swallowing, I said, "Elizabeth, you know all about me, but I know nothing of you."

"What do you want to know?"

"Well, for starters, where are you from?"

"Texas."

I waited for some elaboration. None came, so I asked, "What were your parents like?"

Keyes carefully laid down her fork and sat there staring at her plate for a long minute. When she finally raised her head, her facial expression was cold but her eyes were like red-hot lasers boring through me. "What if I'm an orphan?"

"Are you?"

"What difference does it make to you?" she snapped.

"Um, none, I just, I was just . . ." I stammered. "I'm sorry. I didn't mean to upset you."

"No, I'm sorry. It's a long story, and opening that book just opens up old wounds," she said. "I'd rather talk about how I can help you to clear your name."

"That's kind of you, but why are—"

"You helped me, now I'm helping you." Her smile returned as suddenly as it had disappeared.

Before I could respond, the dusty grandfather clock in the corner chimed six times and Keyes sprung out of her chair.

"Gotta run!" she said. "I'll be back in a couple hours. Just make yourself at home. When I get back, we can talk about your case."

She rushed out of the apartment, grabbing a leather backpack from a hook by the door on her way out.

I sat there in a daze while a cacophony of thoughts prayed on my mind. By midnight Keyes was still not home, and I was exhausted. I stripped to my boxers and climbed into bed, falling into a deep sleep, seconds after my head hit the pillow.

24

Washington, DC
10:00 p.m.

THE TWO CIA CASE officers took the expensive cab ride to the Naked Monkey Bar, a DC hot spot where Omar Farok was known to mingle when he was in town. If everything went according to plan, Farok would soon be in their custody.

But his bodyguards were always by his side, and they were brutal. Recruited from the Republic of the Congo, they came from the ranks of the rebels who'd fought in the Second Congo War, where they'd treated their prisoners with extreme cruelty. These were trained and experienced torturers. They knew how much injury they could inflict on a human body without killing their victim, frequently removing the victim's organs and eating them, a ritualistic practice reflecting their tribe's cannibalistic past. Torture of Farok's girlfriends was a common thing.

At midnight, Farok slipped out of the Naked Monkey

Bar, and headed back to his rented townhouse. He walked briskly toward his destination, only four blocks away. He didn't notice the two CIA operatives who were following him until he was within two blocks of the townhouse. He rarely went anywhere without bodyguards, but that night, he'd felt confidant. He'd misjudged. He'd been a fool to send his guards away.

Farok rarely used his cell phone because there were too many electronic ears listening, waiting for him to slip up. But this was an emergency. He pressed "1" on his speed dial, and made an immediate connection.

"I have company. Two of them," he said quietly. "I'm two blocks away, on M Street by Connecticut Avenue. Take them before they take me."

Four men in black suits and starched white shirts without ties raced from their room to a limo parked at the curb for quick departure. Within a minute, they were behind the two CIA operatives trailing their boss. The limo slowed. Two of the bodyguards jumped from the car, crept up behind the CIA men, and slammed ten-inch jambiyas into their backs, just left of the spine. The attackers thrust upward and then sideways, carving gaping holes into the aorta and heart. As the agents fell forward, the Congolese killers grabbed them under their arms and dragged them to the limo. They shoved the bodies into the back and jumped in.

The limo sped down the street until it caught up to

Farok, then it slowed almost to a stop alongside him. The front passenger door swung open and Farok jumped into the car. While the car raced to a parking garage two blocks away, the rebels removed the cell phones from the pockets of the dead men, wiped off the blood, and handed them to Farok. "We're leaving tonight," Farok said in a quiet voice. "I want to be closer to the target when Celena locates it."

25

Keyes' Apartment
Jackson City, North Carolina
7:45 a.m.

 I WOKE IN A cold sweat, heart racing, disoriented. It took me a minute to get my bearings. I pulled on my clothes and walked down the short hall to the bathroom. The door to Keyes' bedroom was closed, but I could hear her snoring softly inside. *Must've been a late night.*

After getting cleaned up, I went to the kitchen to make some coffee and breakfast. Except for a few bottles of water, some condiments, and a moldy cantaloupe, the refrigerator was pretty much bare, so I walked to the corner market to pick up a few groceries.

An hour later, I was lifting one of my specialties, a veggie frittata, out of the oven when Keyes walked in. Laughing, she said, "You clean and cook? What more could a girl want?"

"It's the least I can do."

I looked into her sparkling eyes. They were inviting. I wanted to touch her, but controlled myself and forced my thoughts back to business mode. Keyes seemed sincere, and God knows I could use an ally.

After breakfast, Keyes gave me a lift to Jackson City Hospital. I still had a license to practice medicine and hospital privileges. I just needed a space to operate and to have access to special equipment for wound care for my post-op patients. I dreaded having to go there because to do so I had to get Herb Waters' approval. It would have been tough enough even before I was accused of murder, but now it would be next to impossible. With everything at stake, I had to give it a try.

Herb Waters ruled the hospital with an iron fist. I went directly to his sixth-floor Penthouse office.

In what little spare time I had, over the previous few months, I'd done research on Waters and the Jackson City Hospital. My research concluded with a half-page op-ed piece that was published in the *Daily Chronicle*, the city paper. In my article, I accused Waters of negotiating to sell our community not-for-profit hospital to the large for-profit conglomerate, American Hospital Systems (AHS). AHS bought and managed hundreds of hospitals all over the United States.

I'd written the piece because the concept of charitable medical care was near and dear to my heart. The purpose of a nonprofit hospital was to provide medical care to all who needed it, not only to those with good insurance or loads of cash in the bank, as was the standard practice at for-profit hospitals. Most physicians had, as I did, a few indigent patients they treated for free, and they relied on the community hospital to accept those patients who needed in-hospital services.

Waters had written a three-column rebuttal to my article. In his piece, which appeared on the front page of the newspaper a few days after my letter was published, Waters repeatedly stated that, "this hospital is not for sale to anyone." Further, he claimed, "Dr. James' letter was written with no knowledge of fact."

I knew that to be a lie because I had personally talked with an AHS executive in Houston four times during the previous month. Waters had never accepted criticism well, and he was beyond livid about my op-ed piece in the newspaper.

Until our recent falling out, Waters and I had been close friends, going back to our freshman year in high school. These days, our relationship was rocky, at best. But I had no choice but to ask for his help.

Herb Waters' office, occupying one-fourth of the roof space of the sixth floor, looked as if it had been dropped from the sky on top of an otherwise functionally well-designed hospital. It was planned by his advisers, who felt he should be physically present at the hospital and not several miles away in the Hanover building, where his office was formerly situated. Hospital employees gave the office the name, "Penthouse," which by common usage became the official title of the structure.

The Penthouse's appearance was questioned by professional builders and designers, even though it was drawn by the best architects in the southeast. Passersby thought that the odd structure was the top of the elevator shafts or the ventilation system. With the Penthouse addition, Waters moved, permanently, from the Hanover building to the hospital, and his title was changed to President of Jackson City Healthcare Systems Inc.

The hospital elevator only went as high as the fifth floor. This was because Waters didn't want to see any of the doctors, and made it difficult for us to reach his office by distancing himself from the hospital complex with a flight of stairs. I took the elevator to the fifth floor and ran up the stairs, bounding into the Penthouse.

I walked into Waters' office reception area. No one other than his private secretary was allowed in Waters' Penthouse.

I surprised the secretary, Shirley Moss. "I need to see your boss."

"Dr. James, please ... I'm not sure if ... " was her tentative response. She looked at me and continued, her voice now firm, "He's busy. You'll have to make an appointment."

I just smiled, lifted the phone, and put it in her hands. "Shirley, can you please make an appointment for me—*now*?"

Waters heard the demand through the closed door and lifted the phone before it rang.

"Dr. James ... is here ... to see you," the receptionist said.

"What? Does he want to kill me now, too?" He yelled so loud that I could easily hear him. "Tell him I'm busy!"

I shouted through the wall, "You have her block for you now? Be a man, Herb—open the door."

Waters threw open his office door and marched to within two feet of me.

I leaned toward Waters, our faces nearly touching.

Waters towered over me. "What the hell are you doing here?"

I looked into the black searing eyes of the man. "My OR will be closed for a few days and I need space to see follow-ups and perform scheduled surgery."

"Goddamn it, Scott. You almost kill your own employee, so then you take out your anesthesiologist and now you want me to let you into my hospital? It'll be a cold day in Hell before you work here again."

"I'll pay your exorbitant hospital costs."

"Yeah, right. You're not seeing any of your patients in my hospital. Tell your patients you're going to Hawaii for a week."

"My patients need hospital services. You don't own the hospital and you have no authority to refuse them."

"Oh yeah? Watch me." He lifted a phone to call security.

My cell phone rang. It was Pete Harris. "I'd like you to come over to my office as soon as possible," he said. "I want to talk to you about hospital finance."

I hung up, then said, "No need to call your henchmen, Herb. I'm leaving."

26

Jackson City Police Station
11:00 a.m.

 WHEN I GOT THERE, Harris was standing just inside the door to his office. He turned his head toward me and stared into my eyes.

"Look," I said, feeling defensive, "if this is about Carey or Keyes, I want a lawyer—"

"Relax, Dr. James. I just wanna talk about the hospital," he said. "Come in and have a seat. You take anything in your coffee?"

"Cream."

Harris pressed the intercom button on his phone, "Jody, could you bring in two cups of coffee, one with cream."

Harris leaned his chin on his hand and just sat there studying me for a long minute. Finally, he said, "Have ya ever considered being a detective?"

"You offering me a job? I could use one, being as I'm shut out of my practice—"

"Doesn't pay as well as plastic surgery, but ya seem to

have a knack for it."

"Should I go out and buy myself a Sherlock Holmes hat and pipe?"

"Ahem … I read through your research notes for your op-ed piece in the *Chronicle*."

"Probably should've never sent that in."

"Well, you make a convincing argument. And your research is very thorough."

"I'm nothing if not thorough. I used to drive my nurses and wife crazy."

"What made ya start lookin' up all that stuff on the hospital in the first place?"

I rubbed my eyes. I wasn't sure where this was leading, but I'd rather have Harris as a friend than an enemy, so I told him the short version of my story. "I came back to town in 2002 after my surgical residency. I wanted to be close to my dad in his twilight years. As you know, we had a little farm that I pretty much ran until I had to go away for my surgical training. Even then, I still came back. Dad sold the tobacco farm and moved to a nursing home, and gave me the money from the sale to set up my practice. Back then, Herb Waters and I were the best of friends. I used to go visit him in his office. Within a year, hospital prices started sky-rocketing, and he got irritated every time I asked him to lower them. He said no one else complained."

"How's that?" Harris asked.

"Herb didn't get it or care. It just pissed him off."

Harris asked in his raspy voice, "Why'd Waters raise the prices so high?"

"To make the hospital more profitable. The board kept raising prices to improve the margins, and then they started adding charges to patients' bills. Things like a toothbrush, a bar of soap, a dietary consultation, and bedside oxygen used to be free, but after Waters took over, everything in the hospital was given a significant charge. He even stopped free coffee for the on-duty doctors and nurses."

"And that made you mad," Harris said rather than asked.

"It didn't make me happy. Listen, Waters is trying to sell the Jackson City Hospital, and I assure you, it's not because he gives a shit about providing better hospital services to the public. It's about lining the pockets of Waters and his partners in crime."

"Maybe. But how does that affect you? You've got a private practice, or rather had a practice and your own surgery center. Why stick your neck out?"

"It's just my nature. People are getting screwed. I had to say something. That's the way my dad raised me."

The detective sucked the molten brew between his teeth. Then he said, "Well, I'm sure that letter ya wrote to the paper pissed off a lot of people at the hospital. Knowin' the temperament of your old buddy Herbie, ya should've expected repercussions. He's not someone ta fuck with."

"Sure, a little negative press makes for bad blood between old friends, but that's no reason to kill someone."

"*Kill* someone? You're saying that Herb Waters murdered those two—"

"Yes. I am. I think it's certainly *possible*. Herb Waters wants to shut me up—"

"*What?* Enough to commit *two murders*?"

"Hell, yes! I can't put my finger on it but Waters is up to something illegal. He's using the hospital for something. There's probably a smoking gun somewhere."

"But why would Waters kill Boyd Carey?"

"I don't believe anybody wanted to kill Dr. Carey. I think they were after me, but encountered Carey instead. He got the needle instead of me. Which is just as good as murdering me, apparently, because now I might be going to jail for life, or worse."

"Hmmm," Harris responded. "I don't know, Doc. That's pretty thin."

"Yeah, well, do your job and investigate Herb Waters!"

"Ha! I can't. It's *way* too thin. Frankly, it sounds a little crazy. To open an investigation, I'd need to show just cause. Right now, I've got squat."

After a long pause, as if throwing me a bone, he said, "But let me know if you find out anything."

"What *I* find? Isn't that your job? Can't you just subpoena documents and statements from Waters and whoever else could be involved in a scam?"

"We have absolutely nothing at all to connect Herb Waters to any murder. Frankly, I'd be embarrassed to go in front of the judge to ask for a warrant." He paused. "Of course, I'm not the one who needs information. You are."

That statement pissed me off. I laughed bitterly at the ridiculousness of the suggestion. "Look, Detective, I'm a plastic surgeon. I'm not a private investigator. You want me to fix your nose? No problem. I can give you a classic Roman—like frickin' Tom Cruise. But investigating a murder? No way. Not my bag."

"Suit yerself, Doc," Harris said. "But if I were facing murder one and attempted murder charges, I'd be makin' like Jason Bourne tryin' ta save my ass."

His words hit me like a sucker punch to the gut. Grunting, I stood to leave. As I turned to walk away, Harris said, "By the way, I told the guards you're allowed access to your office now."

"Thanks," I said with a wave of my hand, not turning back or breaking stride. *At least I'll have somewhere to crash tonight.*

27

The Penthouse, Jackson City Hospital
Jackson City, North Carolina
3:11 p.m.

 HERB WATERS WAS PLAYING a video game and racking up points when the security buzzer went off. "Hold your fucking horses," he yelled. "I'll be there in a minute!"

He was at 48,000 points, trying to break his personal record of 50,000. One last obstacle to beat, and the game was his. Ignoring the door buzzer, he clutched the joysticks even tighter and madly worked the controls, his face and body contorting from the effort. *Bam!* He hit the target! 52 K! "Yes!" he cackled. "I'm the king of the fucking world!"

Waters went to the door and greeted Friedman and Phillips with a diabolical grin on his face and with slaps on their backs. Despite being annoyed with Waters for being slow in letting them in, the two hospital administrators were pleased to see their boss in a good mood. Waters could be impossible to work with when he was upset.

The Missile Game

It had been four weeks since Friedman and Phillips had last seen Waters. Usually they met with him weekly, except when Waters was out of town on business, but for the past six months, the meetings had been reduced to once a month. This wasn't a problem, as Friedman and Phillips were adept at running the hospital and its subsidiaries on their own. But Waters liked to keep a dictatorial control on everything.

Harley Friedman and Craig Phillips were the same age, forty-three, but that's where their similarity ended. Friedman looked like a college professor: balding head with tufts of reddish brown hair around his oversized ears, oversized black glasses with thick lenses, wrinkled shirt, bow tie, sports jacket, and baggy trousers. Of average height, he had rounded shoulders, skinny legs, and a bulging belly. In sharp contrast, Phillips could have graced the cover of *GQ Magazine*: six feet tall, thick wavy hair he kept fashionably styled and neatly trimmed, the "pretty" face of a leading man, and the buffed physique of a professional athlete. Obsessed with exercise, Phillips had a well-equipped gym in his Hanover Building office that he used three or four times a day. He wore sweats most of the time, changing to Brooks Brothers suits and crisply starched shirts when he left his office.

Phillips laid papers over the twenty-foot-long, mahogany table, while Friedman rattled off the main talking points. As always, he kept it brief and made it quick.

Waters had no patience for timidity and little time to discuss hospital business. Despite his reputation as being a goof-off in college, he was extremely smart and a fast study. He grasped and retained information well, and he had a keen ability to quickly connect the dots and see the big picture. Waters was always quick to assess the financial status of Jackson City Hospital, and although his remarks were few, they were always spot-on.

"Why are revenues down for hospital bed usage?" Waters barked.

Friedman was quick to answer. "We had a number of patients cancel due to Dr. James stalking his office manager in the ICU and the two murders at his—"

"That's ancient history," Waters interrupted. "The new contract with Blue Sky has been operational for five weeks. The twenty percent increase in hospital services payments is on-line now. That additional revenue should more than compensate for the eighteen percent drop in bed vacancy for the same period."

"But the increase in charges takes time to reach our ledgers."

"Bullshit!" Waters bellowed as he slammed his fist on the table. "Craig, get Harley straight on this."

Phillips, always the cool head, spoke calmly and confidently. "The twenty percent increase does override the eighteen-point-aught-three percent loss, which works out to

114

a net gain of 143,000 dollars and 15 cents."

Waters maintained a stern look but inwardly he was pleased, not only with the $143,000, but also the 15 cents. Accounting for every last penny was important to Waters.

"Yes, but the money isn't in the hospital account yet," Friedman explained. "It takes a couple days for funds to transfer from the insurance carrier to the hospital."

"We own the goddamned insurance company! It's fuckin' ours! Claims should be expedited! And funds should transfer instantaneously!" Waters fumed. Although no one could tell from his demeanor, he loved these parlays. "The public doesn't judge us on how well our insurance company does; we're judged on the performance of the hospital."

Friedman took the jabs Waters meted out. He was resilient, knowing that his ten percent of Jackson Healthcare Systems, Inc.'s profits, like Phillips', would be over sixteen million dollars for the quarter.

At the conclusion of the meeting, Waters announced he would be out of touch for the next three weeks. "Don't need me," he barked. Then he dismissed them curtly with, "I have to make an important phone call."

Waters waited for Phillips and Friedman to leave by the stairs and exit the Penthouse, then went to his luxurious bathroom to shower and shave.

Freshly bathed, Waters stretched out naked on the Penthouse's king-sized bed and adjusted the pillows so he could sit up and watch television. He turned on the secured video-conferencing program he often used. The seventy-inch screen filled with a live feed of a naked woman lying on a large round bed with two cheetahs. Wind blew sheer drapes, showing glimpses of azure water outside the window. The animals sat rigidly upright, like the sphinxes standing guard at an ancient Egyptian pyramid, poised and attentive to the woman's fondling.

The woman, like the animals, was exquisitely beautiful. She said not a word as she seductively gestured for him to come to her. She slithered on the satin sheets and licked her full lips to form wet kisses directed toward the camera. Silently observing her graceful movements, Waters became sexually aroused. When she licked her fingers and began caressing herself, he took his penis in his hand. Soon they were on their respective beds, panting, spent, while the big cats, still motionless, purred.

Finally, she sat up and said, "I miss you, darling. You haven't called in over a week. Are you seeing someone else?"

"Elayna, baby, you're the only girl in my life right now."

"Good. I like it that way. Come see me soon. I'll make it worth your while."

Waters said, "It'll be three weeks before I can get away."

28

Scott James Surgery Center
3:45 p.m.

 AFTER LEAVING HARRIS, KEYES drove me to my office.

My heart sank as we pulled into the parking lot of the surgery center. The side of the building had KILLER DOCTOR spray-painted on it, in three-foot-high letters. At least my building was a few blocks away from the hospital. Along with the trees, that gave it some degree of privacy.

Not only had vandals painted my wall, they'd wrecked my car. There was my Mercedes, covered in red and blue spray paint, with KILLER DOC painted on the windshield. The windows were smashed and the leather seats slashed. The tires and stereo system were gone.

Two teenagers, skateboarding in the parking lot, ducked behind the building just as I got out of Keyes' Honda. As I unlocked my office door, the two yelled, "Cop killer!" and ran toward the nearby apartments. I looked for a policeman, but Harris had removed them all and I was alone.

A mound of mail greeted me as I entered the office. I went immediately to the waiting room to check my orchids. Now that my practice was dead, my flowers were dying, too. Many of the blooms had fallen off and the soil was bone dry. Most of the water in the small pool I had designed to keep the orchids healthy had evaporated. It was too low to keep the waterfall going, and the motor had burned out.

Orchids are the diamonds of cut flowers. So prized are they for their beauty, they are the most commonly used flowers for corsages, bouquets, and floral arrangements. The sweet smell of the aromatic orchid will last until the flower wilts. After two weeks, my orchids had lost most of their life.

I walked past the waiting room and took the mail to my office, where I sat in my chair and picked out a dozen handwritten letters, hoping to find one that would pick me up. Three were from patients praising my work and expressing sadness for the false accusations—all saying, in so many words, "We believe in you."

I sorted out the bills. I knew from previous months that they would total over $30,000. Alicia had taken the money earmarked to cover these costs. There were no funds in any of my accounts, and I had no surviving credit card accounts as back up.

After tossing a dozen or so advertisements in the trash can, I turned to the mail I'd been saving for last: One envelope from Family Court and one from the North Carolina Board of Medicine. My heart sank as I read the first letter: an order forbidding me from seeing my children.

Gritting my teeth, I opened the second letter and began to read: "The North Carolina Board of Medicine has determined that your felony charges make you unfit to practice medicine in this state. You will cease and desist providing surgical and non-surgical care."

Unable to read another word, I tore the letter into small pieces. Then I put my head on the desk and cried. I'd read about other people being depressed, but I'd never really felt depression, myself, before now. I'd always thought depression was something for mentally weak individuals, not people like me. I'd always been in charge of others and in control of my emotions. Depression became real to me during my stint in jail.

I missed, most of all, my kids. I really wanted to see them, but Alicia wouldn't allow it. She wouldn't even let me to talk to them on the phone. I was worried about the effect all this was having on them. Their mother seemed to believe the vicious lies about me, so my marriage was probably over. And there was a good chance I was going to a penitentiary for a crime I didn't commit.

It became crystal clear to me that I had no future.

I walked to the hallway where Officer Wilson had been shot and looked at the bloodstains—now dried—that had dripped down the wall and then pooled on the carpet, after the bullet had ripped through the doomed man's skull.

Oh, God, I'm going to be convicted, and I'm going to get the death penalty. I'm a dead man.

The loss of my children and the loss of my medical license gave me a real sense of futility. Bankruptcy was certain, and that was the least of my problems. I'd been charged with two murders and an attempted murder, and I had no defense. The prosecutor was asking for the death penalty, as the local newspaper had reported, and the crimes were so horrific that the jury would probably grant it. At least my death would be painless. Since the gas chamber was eliminated in North Carolina in 1998, the only available execution method was lethal injection.

I was very familiar with the procedure. I had advocated for it in 2001, and had even gone to legislative sessions in Raleigh, where I'd testified to lawmakers about how animals were humanely put to death whereas cruel and torturous methods were used on humans. It looked like I would become a benefactor of the legislation I had promoted.

29

Transcript:
House Select Committee on Sentencing Guidelines
North Carolina State Senate March, 2002

DR. SCOTT JAMES:

"Ours is a merciful society, a society that values the rights of all our citizens, even the criminals who refuse to live by our moral values. In the worst of crimes, our state provides for the death penalty. But this capital punishment should not be a vengeful infliction of pain during execution."

SEN. HON. E.G. HIGGINS:

"Dr. James. We welcome your testimony. I have a comment I'd like to make, if I may. My daughter was brutally raped and tortured until she died. You want to put our hardest criminals to sleep, like a mother rocking her child at night."

Dr. S. James:

"Uhm. No, Senator."

Sen. Hon. E.G. Higgins:

"Are you volunteering to sing a lullaby as well?"

Dr. S. James:

"An early form of social justice was instituted by the French in 1792, the Guillotine. By this, the commoners were executed by the same instrument used on noblemen. This helped quiet a restless society. And we have a restless society today."

Sen. Hon. T.W. Williams:

"Dr. James. You're talking about … What did you say, 'social justice,' I believe? These criminals are dogs. They're *dogs!* They should be stomped!"

<u>30</u>

Scott James Surgery Center
4:18 p.m.

I DIDN'T WANT TO be "stomped."

The same drugs the state of North Carolina now used to execute criminals were in my pharmaceutical cabinet. I could end it all now and save myself the anguish and humiliation of going through a trial and sitting on death row, waiting for the state's executioner to kill me.

I walked swiftly to the OR, knocking over a chair and any equipment that blocked my path to the med cabinet. It was locked and I had no key. I pounded its door with my fist until I drew blood, then tore an arm board from the operating table and slammed it into the cabinet door. But the steel and tempered-glass was too strong and didn't break.

Going to another cabinet, I raked surgical instruments and supplies to the floor, throwing aside delicate tools until I found a heavy, surgical mallet, and the osteotomes I used to fracture and move facial bones. With my skill and these instruments, I could create a facial structure that met my mandate for perfection. Now, I'd use them to ensure my own perfect death. I wedged the one-inch-wide osteotome in the door of the locked drug cabinet, made one sharp rap with the mallet, and the door flew open. I knocked bottles of pills and vials of liquid medications to the tile floor in my frenzied search for the right drugs: Sodium Pentothal for sleep and succinyl-choline for death.

My hands shook as I ripped open the packages and filled two syringes, one with Pentothal, the other with succinyl-choline. After placing the IV line, I inserted a Y-connector and secured the two syringes to it. I inserted the needle into a vein and withdrew the syringe's plunger. I got a strong back-flow of blood

The needle was in a large, stable vein. There was no room for error. I had to inject the Pentothal as fast as I could and quickly shoot in the muscle-paralyzing succinyl-choline before the Pentothal induced sleep.

Then I would have a painless death.

My rambling mind thought of orchids. The Satyrium pumilum is called the "death flower." It originated on the burial islands off Madagascar. Some Malagasy ethnic groups traditionally left their dead in designated areas to decompose in the open air, which aided in the evolutionary development of orchids with blooms that smell like decayed meat. These orchids attract pollinator flies and beetles that feed on the dead.

I needed to die. That was my only escape. I put the palm of my hand on the plunger of the Pentothal syringe, took a deep breath, and pushed it hard. The liquid coursed rapidly through my vein. My head whirled, and I fell to the floor.

Quickly, I shifted my hand to the syringe of succinyl-choline and pressed the plunger. Visual auras darted before me and I saw my parents, my children, and the faces of many patients. I felt myself floating and saw sparkling white trees swaying below me. As life ebbed from my body with each dying beat of my heart, I was engulfed in a bright white light filled with beautiful children, laughing and dancing, dressed in white. Suddenly, a white orchid appeared at my side. I took it in my hand and held it.

Finally, everything was peaceful and perfect once again.

31

Drone Control Center, "Alpha Charlie"
Jackson City, North Carolina
4:31 p.m.

CHARLIE PUT ON HIS headset and flipped the switch. "Colonel Edwards, are you with me?"

"Yes sir, Alpha Charlie."

"Do we have a secure voice transmission?"

"Affirmative, sir. Be advised. Most of our Kandahar crew is now in Iraq, much closer to our new mission."

"Do you have targets spotted right now?"

"Negative. We're just going to perform the laser test today."

"Understood."

Edwards had already launched the MQ-1 from Peary. The Predator was flying over Virginia, waiting to test Weizman's laser. Edwards instructed Charlie to sacrifice one of the government's remote-control Jeeps in a practice field in Fort Eustis. Located thirty miles from Camp Peary, along the James River near Newport News, Fort Eustis was the U.S. Army's transportation center.

Edwards' voice came back on in the headset, "Are you all set for the test?"

"Roger that."

Homeland Security was anxious to have the laser-equipped Predator ready for service in the skies over America, and Weizman was anxious to confirm that his laser could function on the aircraft as well as it had in his California laboratory. If the laser worked, a Hellfire missile would be his next test target. Successfully killing a Hellfire in mid-flight with the laser was a realistic goal for Weizman, or so he thought, and would open the gates for a laser defense system that could stop in-coming intercontinental ballistic missiles.

Charlie looked over his chair and identified the controls. When his chair had first arrived, Weizman had taken special pride in informing him that the laser controls were tucked underneath and out of the way. They could be activated simply by voice command. Charlie had worked with the voice recognition software for all of ten minutes before the computer understood him perfectly.

Charlie said, now, aloud: "Dee Eee controls."

Two joysticks slowly rose from below the seat of the chair.

"Everything feels good," Charlie told Edwards. "Give

me your best figure-eight with the robotic Jeep."

The drone flew at 30,000 feet over Camp Peary. The sighting was not as difficult as Weizman had led him to believe. Charlie concentrated and put the sights carefully on the swerving jeep, then fired. A brilliant white light rose from the hood. Charlie felt like he was looking into a camera's flash, one that went off continuously for ten seconds. The jeep immediately went out of control and then flipped over in a huge cloud of dust. The laser fried the vehicle's fuel injectors, alternator, fuel pump, onboard engine computer— *everything*. The intense heat melted the vinyl seats and then set the entire jeep on fire. The explosion that followed was not very impressive. There was only a gallon of fuel in the gas tank, per governmental agency frugality.

The jeep lay dead now, with a huge plume of black smoke billowing from its flaming hulk.

Colonel Edwards congratulated him. "Excellent shot, Mr. W—"

"CHARLIE!"

Alpha Charlie jumped to his feet before Edwards finished his sentence. Glaring at Edwards in the monitor, he said in a low, threatening tone. "You will refer to me only as 'Charlie.' My name is never to be said to anyone—not to your co-workers, the other drone operators, the officers in your unit—not even to the President of the United States."

"Sorry, sir. It was a slip-up. It'll never happen again … Charlie."

"Colorado State Legislature Bans Civilian Drone Ops"
DENVER POST

DENVER, CO THE STATE Legislature has passed a resolution prohibiting the placement of civilian drone control centers in the state of Colorado. At odds with the Air Force's huge presence in the state, the legislative body has taken the token step of bringing a non-binding bill to the floor. Colorado State Senator, Frank Teig, sponsor of the bill, said, after the vote, "We're aware of the fact that there aren't any civilian contractors working in the U.S., but in light of recent attacks, we just wanted to make an important statement."

32

Scott James Surgery Center
5:11 p.m.

"SCOTT," KEYES CALLED OUT, as she entered the waiting room. "Scott!"

She moved quickly through the office. Reaching the OR, she stopped dead in her tracks. A chair had been smashed against a wall and the Bovie electrocautery machine was on its side on the floor. An instrument table was upside down and lying on the anesthesia cart. Surgical instruments, medications, and supplies were strewn all over the countertops and floor.

Keyes raced to the recovery room and screamed when she saw James' body on the floor. She kneeled and felt for a pulse. It was weak, almost imperceptible. In a moment of uncertainty, she paused before slapping his cheeks, hard. "Scott! Wake up!" There was no response. His face was pale gray.

Keyes placed her lips on his, squeezed his nostrils shut, and began blowing air into his lungs as hard as she could. His body twitched. She compressed his chest several times, and then resumed the mouth-to-mouth resuscitation. After her first blow, he tried to breathe, but his airway was obstructed. Keyes shoved her hand deep down his throat and mopped out thick mucous. He inhaled with the heavy snore of a partial blockage.

Bottles and vials of medications were scattered all around. She recognized the empty succinyl-choline bottle and sighed relief at the large volume of unused medication still in the syringe in his arm. He'd injected less than 1 cc; the lethal dose was 5 cc. She jerked the syringe from the IV and threw it against the wall. She quickly looked at the labels on the drug vials, throwing them aside until she had the one she wanted: Narcan. It was a potent drug that reversed the actions of sedatives. She drew 10 cc in a syringe and stuck it his vein. She injected half of it, paused briefly, then shrugged and injected the entire bolus.

She used a catheter to suction the back of his throat and trachea, removing gobs of thick, white mucous. He started breathing easier.

She wiped the tears from her eyes and dragged James over to the anesthesiology machine. It was connected to three tanks: oxygen, nitrous oxide, and air. Holding his chin up, she put her mouth over his and blew her breath into his lungs six times. Then she fumbled with gas lines and placed the oxygen mask on James' face. She grabbed the black balloon and squeezed as hard as she could. No oxygen moved into his lungs. The airway was still blocked.

Her heart pounded fast in her chest. She'd read about all these maneuvers and helped others do them several times in Houston, but never before had she performed them by herself.

Removing the mask, Keyes again reached her small hand deeply down his throat. His tongue was inverted. The succinyl-choline had relaxed the tongue and it had fallen back in the pharynx and was choking him. She pulled it back into his mouth. With trembling hands, she placed a plastic airway in his mouth to push the tongue forward. She quickly reattached the mask and squeezed the bag as hard as she could with both hands. Success! His lungs filled with air! Sweat dripped from her face and covered her entire body.

She sat on the floor beside James for half an hour, rhythmically inflating his lungs.

33

Scott James Surgery Center
7:30 p.m.

I WAS LYING ON the hard tile floor of the operating room. I tried to swallow. My throat was so painful, I gagged. My lungs burned with each breath.

Putting my hand to my mouth, I coughed and felt a tingling sensation in my arm. I looked and saw that my entire forearm had ballooned out from an infiltrated IV of D-5½ normal saline. Reaching down, I jerked the malfunctioning needle from my arm. The cold liquid running from the IV saturated my shirt.

Then something moved beside me. I turned, and there was Elizabeth Keyes, lying next to me on the floor, staring at me.

"Hey," she said.

"Hey."

"Let me put that back in for you." She studiously reattached the IV, then said, "Welcome back. I thought I'd lost you." Tears welled in her eyes.

I reached out for her hand, squeezed it and then kissed it. "I thought I was in heaven when I looked up and saw your face. An angel, that's what you are."

"An angel, huh?"

"No. A hundred angels, for all you did for me."

She took a deep breath and then asked, "You feeling okay?"

"Yeah. I'll live . . . " I smiled.

"Not funny, mister," she said, looking deeply into my eyes and not returning the smile. "You're not gonna try that again, right?"

"No. I'm good. Especially if you stay with me."

34

Keyes' Apartment
1:14 p.m.

 I OPENED MY EYES and saw Elizabeth beside me, in bed, in her guest room.

I'd slept restlessly since we'd returned to the apartment in the early afternoon. Each time I woke up, I'd look for Keyes, who was always at my side, smiling. Twice she kissed my forehead. I tried to stay awake, but kept drifting off. With our medical backgrounds, we both knew my somnolence was the result of the large quantity of Pentothal I'd injected into my body. Ironically, the Pentothal had saved my life. It knocked me out so fast that I was asleep before I could inject a lethal dose of the succinyl-choline. I did get enough of the muscle-paralyzing agent into my body to cause all over muscle fatigue, a "sometimes" side effect patients describe after the agent is used in surgery.

"Thanks for saving me," I said when I awoke.

"Next time you wanna say 'good-bye,' do it with a Post-it note or something."

She left the bed and went to start making dinner.

As we ate, Keyes told me she had some errands to run. She also expressed her concern for the state of my physical and mental health. She said I still seemed sluggish, and she asked me pointed questions about my depression. I agreed I still felt achy and fatigued, but I assured her I had no compulsion to do the suicide bit again. No, I wouldn't do anything further to harm myself. Yes, I promised to remain in bed if she went out.

As we were eating, there was suddenly a loud knock on the apartment door, so loud that it startled me and I jumped a little in my chair.

But Keyes was unfazed. Without a word of explanation she got up, went to open the door, stepped out, and closed the door completely behind her.

The stairwell was lit and visible from the living room window. I got up and stood just behind the curtain and peered out. Keyes was standing face to face with a woman with tousled black hair, dark sunglasses, and a deeply tanned face. She had the same hourglass figure as Keyes but was a couple of inches taller. A heavy cardboard tube lay against the wall of the apartment. It was the type typically used to carry architecture plans or nautical charts. After a brief conversation that I couldn't hear, the woman handed Keyes the brown cardboard cylinder, then walked briskly down the stairs and out of sight.

I ran back to the hallway, cut back inside the kitchen, and sat down just as she came back in.

After she closed the door, I walked into the living room and asked, "Everything okay?"

"Yeah."

"Was that your friend? Was that Anna—Anna Duke?"

"Uhm ... No. That was someone else."

"What did she bring you?" I said.

"It's personal." She suddenly grew weary. *God, she looks tired. Like the weight of the world is on her shoulders.*

I felt the overwhelming desire to help her. I said, "I truly appreciate everything you've done for me. You saved my life, for Christ's sake! ... Is there anything I can do for you?"

Her tears began to flow. I put my arm around her, trying to console her, but she only stiffened.

"Yes, there is," she finally said. "There is something you can do for me. I'll tell you . . . later. But only if you promise you'll do whatever I ask—no matter what it is."

"The consequences of noncompliance?"

"Death," she said quietly.

I laughed, but she didn't smile. She wasn't joking.

"Uhm, well ... Remember, I'm suicidal, so dying is not a problem for me."

That almost brought her smile back, but she just stood there looking at me and waiting.

I hadn't given my promise.

"Promise," I said softly.

"C'mon, let's tuck you in." Taking me by the hand, she led me back to the bedroom and softly pushed me back on the bed. "Oh, I forgot something," she said. "I'll be right back."

She returned with a glass of ice water in one hand and a folded newspaper in the other. She put the glass on the nightstand and tossed the *Chronicle* onto the bed beside me. "Reading material," she said.

Within minutes of her departure, I fell asleep.

35

Farmhouse
Ellsbury, North Carolina
2:31 p.m.

 ELIZABETH KEYES LAID THE cardboard tube on the large table upstairs, and then pulled out the stolen hospital plans. The architectural drawings of the Jackson City Hospital were immense in size and exceedingly complicated. It was virtually impossible to follow the many alterations that had been made to the structure in the past ten years.

The Penthouse was the problem. This was the logical place, Keyes believed, for the location of Alpha Charlie's drone controls, but a dozen different renditions had been drawn.

Taking care of Scott James over the last twenty-four hours had diverted her from actively searching for Alpha Charlie. That wasn't good for her. Her most recently received text had been the most demanding of them all: CELENA, CALL MY NUMBER BY LANDLINE WHEN

CHARLIE IS IN HIS CONTROL SITE. IMMEDIATELY MY MISSILES WILL BE LAUNCHED. IF YOU FAIL, THE REPLACEMENT WILL COME FOR YOU. J.H.

On two separate occasions, Keyes had crawled through the ductwork of the Penthouse and had then entered every room and closet in the sixth-floor suite, but she'd been unable to find the drone controls.

Now she couldn't find them on the drawings, either. Originally, one of the four elevators serving the hospital had opened into the center of the Penthouse. On the latest version of the drawings, however, the elevator going to the Penthouse was closed on all floors except the sub-basement, and inside Waters' private office. The same was true of the backup stairway for that elevator.

After carefully studying all versions of the architectural blueprints of the hospital structure, as well as maps of the surrounding grounds, Keyes had come up empty. There was no sign of a control center, or a place to *hide* a control center. Maybe the initial intelligence she'd received had been wrong.

She'd have to get deeper inside Herb Waters' little fortress, but *virtually*. She began working through all the hacking protocols she'd learned. First, she'd need to find out how to get into the hospital's website.

Then she'd figure out how to get to Herb Waters.

36

The Penthouse, Jackson City Hospital
2:35 p.m.

"GODDAMN IT TO FUCKING hell!" Waters screamed.

Shirley Moss was used to that kind of profane outburst from Waters. But when it was followed by the crashing sound of a chair hitting the wall and his shout to "Get your ass in here!" she knew he was more upset than usual.

Moss walked two steps inside the door and stood there quietly as Waters hovered over his desk. His heavily-creased face was deeply tanned. Shirley suspected his dark brown hair was mostly gray, judging by the bottles of hair coloring that were often in his desk drawer. His massive, well-muscled chest and arms bulged against his always-starched-and-pressed white shirts.

"Someone was here!" Waters yelled. "Who was it?" His face was red and the large veins in his neck and face bulged.

Michael Jefferson, Waters' enormous "security guard," who was much more like a professional intimidator than anything else, waved a silver metal rod over the entry door, the wall around the entry door, and the carpet. A low-frequency hum issued as the rod moved past Waters' office door. The hulking Jefferson turned to look at Waters.

"Goddamn it to fucking hell!" Waters shouted again as he picked a quarter-inch brown "spot" from the door, just above the upper hinge. He shoved it in Shirley's face. The miniature transmitting device looked like a ladybug, with three tiny wires protruding from one end. Waters then ceremoniously threw it on the floor and stomped on it.

"Why would someone want to plant a microphone in your office?" Shirley asked.

"Who the fuck knows?" Waters barked, lying, knowing that there were lots of people who wanted to bug his office, his car, and his home. Shaking his finger at Shirley, he barked, "I don't give a fuck who it is; if you ever let anybody else enter this office, I'll can your ass!"

Shirley looked down and returned to her desk.

37

I WOKE UP THIRSTY, my throat parched. The ice cubes in the glass of water Keyes had left on the nightstand had melted, but the cold water soothed my sore throat. My back was stiff from lying down. It felt good to stand and walk around after being in bed for so long.

The newspaper Keyes had left was creased as if it had been folded for reading. Opening it, I saw the reason she'd left it. There was a two-page ad by Jackson City Hospital with the headline: "Our Hospital is One of the Best in the Southeast: Let Us Serve Your Every Need." The ad copy consisted of two columns listing the names and credentials of the outstanding, board-certified physicians on staff, covering all fields of medicine and surgery. On and on the hospital bragged about their caring, competent service to the community.

Notably missing were any references to any of the

events of the past few weeks.

I was worried about Waters and I knew he was going to sell the hospital. It reminded me that the world was still turning, and that I had to return a phone call.

I called the home of my friend, Andy Fowler, who'd been in a master's program in hospital administration while I was a resident surgeon in plastic surgery. He now worked at American Hospital Systems (AHS), and when I was doing research on the hospital sale the previous month, Andy was my primary source of information. After several unanswered rings, the call went to voicemail, and I left a message. "This is Scott James. I need to talk to Andy as soon as possible. It's important."

A minute later, my cell phone rang and a sobbing Frances Fowler spoke four words before hanging up: "Don't call here. Ever!"

Ten minutes later, my phone rang again. It was Frances Fowler. "I was afraid to talk on the home phone. They're listening to all my calls, so I use my cell phone. I buried Andy three weeks ago. They said it was a heart attack, but I know they killed him."

"I'm sorry, Frances. I had no idea." I was so stunned and devastated to hear of Andy's death that I didn't absorb her last words at first. "Who killed him?"

"They're after me now, and it's your fault!" Frances said. "That letter you wrote to your newspaper led to Andy's death. They told him not to give out any information about AHS buying your hospital. His boss ordered him a month ago not to talk to you. The day after your newspaper article was published, Andy went to work feeling fine. He called me when he got to his office and whispered that he was in big trouble."

Her voice trembled as she spoke through her tears. "He told me he was scared. That he'd been beaten. And if something happened to him, not to call you. He was afraid they'd do something to me. An hour later, I got a call saying he was dead."

"Did you go to the police?"

"Yes. But nobody listened to me because I had three psychiatric visits for... a little problem ... over a year ago, and they found out."

"Who found out?"

"The men Andy worked for. Doctors' records are supposed to be confidential, but they knew of my office visits and that I had two prescriptions for Prozac."

"Didn't the police see the body? If someone beat him, there would have been cuts or bruises."

"No. Andy was cremated—without me first seeing his body and without my consent."

"That's against the law!"

"These people at AHS *are* the law. They own the police, the coroner, even my psychiatrist. I've read about your situation, Scott. Aren't they doing the same thing to you?"

"Yes, Frances, they are. I just need to find out who 'they' are. That's why I was calling—"

She started to cry. "There's one. He's horrible. He was with Andy when he died. His name is Joshua Brightman. He's a scary-looking man, tall, maybe six-five, huge, built like a pro wrestler, with a long stringy ponytail and strange blue eyes that seem to stare right through you."

I couldn't believe my ears. A shot of adrenaline bolted through my veins. "Oh my God. Did you say a huge guy with a blond ponytail?"

Abruptly, her crying ceased. "That's them!" she said. "They're right behind me!"

"Who?"

"A woman and two children! They're following me!"

The connection cut off.

Is Frances Fowler just paranoid? Am I paranoid? Did she just describe the attendant I saw in the ICU leaving Keyes' bedside?

Frantic, I tried calling her back. I tried three times. It was clear she'd turned off her phone.

38

Hangar 4
Camp Peary, Virginia
3:46 p.m.

 THERE WERE MANY MORE targets, and Alpha Charlie was the man to take them out. First, though, he wanted to make the DE Laser operational. Once that was accomplished, the DE system would be transferred to the drones in the Middle East. The afternoon's practice run was important to him.

As Charlie was getting comfortable in his chair, the MQ-1 Predator rolled from its hangar and flew into the air from Camp Peary. At the same time, a remote-controlled Jeep left a helicopter hangar at Fort Eustis, drove slowly away from the airport, past the shooting range, and then down a variety of dirt roads constructed by the base engineers to mimic battlefields. As the Jeep approached an open field surrounded by bunkers, a blue light glowed on the dashboard, signaling that missile targeting radar was surveying the area. Practiced in evasive moves that simulated what an expert driver would do in combat situations, the Jeep's remote control operator accelerated the vehicle and moved it to the center of the field.

The Jeep's brakes slammed on. The vehicle reversed itself.

Charlie sat, impatiently tapping his foot, until an Apache helicopter, hovering roughly five miles away, launched a Hellfire missile aimed at the Jeep.

The light on the Jeep's dashboard changed to red; the Hellfire radar had locked on. The missile would strike in eight seconds. Before it hit, Charlie would have to fire the DE Laser and incinerate it. The laser beam traveled at the speed of light and would strike the target at almost the same time it was fired. The challenge, therefore, was in holding the sights on the fast-moving target.

The Jeep shifted gears and screeched forward, circling the field at thirty miles per hour with the red radar warning light flashing.

Knowing the brevity of his opportunity, Charlie kept his eye on the missile from the second it launched. Weizman's laser had sufficient energy to discharge eight times. In the excitement of his first testing of the system, it took Charlie precious seconds to get his sights on the Hellfire. He felt stiff as he pulled his trigger twice.

And missed.

He sighted and fired four more times, but each time he

was too late. He couldn't score a hit on the Hellfire before it blew up the Jeep—in spectacular computer screen glory.

He had failed.

He pounded the desk with his fist and shouted, "Goddamn it!" into his mic.

Edwards' star trigger man had missed.

Edwards barked out his analysis. "First of all, that Hellfire was moving at Mach 1.3, 950 miles per hour. Even though Weizman thinks his laser will kill at Mach 2, 1,500 miles per hour, that may not be a reality. But before you undercut his prediction, you should practice more with your controls. Practice is something you've done little of, Charlie."

Charlie bristled. He squeezed his fists so tight that his knuckles went white.

Edwards continued. "You overpowered the targeting mechanism. Weizman said the DE controls respond to electrostatic charges of hands near the controls. You should manually sight the gun up to the moment of firing and then ease your hands off to allow the target reference to take over."

Charlie stood and put his face in the camera. "I know what the fuck I'm doing! I wanna try again. Now, get off your ass and recharge the DE. Call me when you're ready!"

39

Keyes' Apartment
3:50 p.m.

THE NEWS OF ANDY'S death unnerved me, to say the least. And the name "Joshua Brightman" echoed in my head. My sole ally in researching Waters' dealings with AHS, Andy Fowler, was dead. Swiftly cremated, in fact. The only people, besides me, who'd ever questioned Herb Waters' management of the Jackson City Hospital, Cabot Barnes and Quinton Jolly, were also dead. Were the deaths truly related? Were they indeed *murders*—all of them? Could Waters' be so desperate to keep things a secret that he would go on a killing spree? He could if he could make it all look like an accident.

My mouth was still dry and still tasted awful, no doubt from the drugs I'd given myself. I brushed my teeth over the kitchen sink, threw some water on my face and combed my hair. I looked around for a razor, but couldn't find one.

I went into Keyes' bedroom, to go to her bathroom. With all the power cables stretched across the floor, connected to a dozen odd-looking electronic boxes, it was difficult to walk without tripping. She was into electronics big time, apparently. Every surface was covered with them.

Brushing past her worktable, I saw a canvas shopping bag filled with documents, lying on its side, next to two TV screens and an electrical circuitry diagram. There were several papers splayed over the carpet beside the bed, too, including some official looking documents that she'd obviously wadded up in anger, and flung off the bed. In the middle of the debris, I saw a page of rough brown stationary, with handwriting on it: "Celena, Bombings resuming in Islamic State. Hormand is ready to proceed. Target must be located soon. Our missiles are ready to fire. Quasart."

I stopped in my tracks.

There was another handwritten message in what looked like Arabic.

I couldn't help but start to look around.

I knelt down and picked up a blurry memo that had been photocopied numerous times. It was from a CIA director in Langley, Virginia: "Terror alert red. Target, Mid-Atlantic region. Pakistani Operatives possibly assisting ISIL/ISIS." It was dated four days ago.

My mind started racing.

I looked nearby for anything that might explain what I was looking at, but found nothing. Standing up, I looked around the room and spotted a shredder next to the dresser, filled with strips of stationary of the same type as the intact message from Quasart. In the jaws of the shredder I found a business card made of a thicker version of the coarsely textured paper. The shredder had chewed away only a third of the card. After flattening the ridges created by the shredding, I could decipher the printed name: "Harold Simpkins," and a phone number. Below it was a handwritten address. It was hard to read, but I finally made it out. It was in Chapel Hill, 4360 Emmaus Church Road. There was another phone number, but I could read only five of the numbers: 919 55. The rest was smudged.

What does Keyes have to do with bombings in Pakistan? Why does Keyes have a CIA memo? Target? I cringed. *What target is this Quasart going to strike?*

40

Keyes' Apartment
4:02 p.m.

 I HAD TO GET out of that apartment. I grabbed the business card from the shredder, went to the guest bedroom, got a few things, and then ran out the door.

I jogged down the street. I didn't know what was happening to my world. After about ten minutes of simply running, I sat down at a bus stop and buried my face in my hands.

I sat there thinking. My life was in the hands of this woman, Elizabeth Keyes. I didn't know her, really, but since I'd gotten out of jail we'd become very close. I couldn't help but feel real affection for her. She'd saved my life. But she'd lied to me, several times, and now something was clearly wrong.

Keyes claimed that she was an experienced medical office manager, that she'd received her training at St. Mary's hospital in Texas. Harold Garner, the chief of the medical technologist program at St. Mary's, had personally written a letter of recommendation for her. I took out my smart phone and began to look up phone listings for the administrator of St. Mary's Hospital. After one ring, the main operator at St. Mary's said, crisply, "Mr. Garner will be with you shortly."

Garner answered on the second ring. He said that Keyes had been in the office manager's program for three weeks, moving into the advanced courses after the first week and making perfect scores on all the exams. She'd even taken night classes in the OR tech school, and after ten days, she'd passed the final exam given to the second-year class.

"No wonder you wrote such a glowing recommendation of her," I said.

"I didn't write a letter of recommendation for Elizabeth Keyes to anyone," Garner responded. He explained that Keyes had spent so little time in his class, he didn't feel qualified to evaluate her.

"But Herb Waters sent me an email. He said it was your personal recommendation."

Garner paused. "It's his hospital. He *owns* Saint Mary's. He can say or do anything he wishes."

Waters owns Saint Mary's?

On a hunch, I asked Garner if he'd ever heard the name "Harold Simpkins."

"Uhm ... It seems like Elizabeth brought a man named Harold to the hospital a few times. But I'm positive she said his last name was Simpson, not Simpkins. He was a small guy, balding a bit. Said he lived in Taylor, Texas, with his mother. I think he was some kind of actor, like a bad TV spokesman or something."

After the conversation with Garner ended, I was no longer sure of anyone or anything. Why had Waters led me to believe that Garner had written Keyes' recommendation? And why had he said Keyes was qualified to be a medical office manager when her training was as a medical technician? It had been the letter of recommendation that had gotten Keyes the job in my office. Why did Waters want Keyes in my office?

I started thinking that I was paranoid, like Frances Fowler, Andy's wife.

I sat staring for a long time at the half-shredded business card. Emmaus Church Road. I searched Google Maps with my phone. It was local — in Chapel Hill, just eighteen some-odd miles away.

Harold Simpkins.

I sat and thought for no more than five minutes.

I walked to one of the nearby strips of thrift shops that dotted Keyes' neighborhood, and with what money I had, bought a cheap mountain bike. I purchased an old baseball cap and sunglasses, as well, and began pedaling to Chapel Hill.

41

Emmaus Church Road
Chapel Hill, North Carolina
6:40 p.m.

THE SKY WAS OVERCAST and the sun was setting as I biked north on Fordham Street and then turned west on Emmaus Church Road. With the waning light and poorly marked houses in this rural area, I had to look hard to find the address, 4360, which was barely visible on the dilapidated mailbox. The yard was so overgrown with small pines and untrimmed hedges that I had a hard time even seeing the house.

I slowly pedaled by the property and saw a dim light in one of the first-story windows. The blinds were partially drawn. I couldn't really make out anything from the street. I kept riding until I reached a dirt road about a quarter mile away, where thick woods stood on both sides and afforded good concealment. I stopped and quickly stashed the bike in a thicket.

I began trekking back toward the house. A hundred

yards short of the property, I left the road and ducked into the tall weeds. I crept up to the house, and, hiding behind an overgrown juniper next to the window, peeked in. The large living room was furnished with only an old sofa, an end table with a small lamp on it, and a television sitting on a crate. The sofa was at an angle in front of the TV, with part of the sofa's back facing the window. I had to position myself at the corner of the window to see who it was that was sitting there. It was a man, reclining on the sofa, and watching TV. He wore a sleeveless undershirt, black boxer shorts, and sandals. He had dark skin and black, closely cropped hair. Lying next to him on the couch was a phone — a landline.

I moved carefully around the exterior of the house, looking in all the other windows, but it was too dark to see in. When I reached the side of the house, I noticed that the door to the detached garage was partly open, and I quickly walked the twenty paces or so over to it. Two vehicles were parked inside: a gold Cadillac and a black pickup. I moved past the Caddy to the Ford F 150, noting its tinted windows, chrome running boards, whitewalls, and fog lights.

The truck faced outward, like it was ready to go. Standing in the dark, letting my eyes adjust, I noticed that mud covered the truck's rear license plate.

A license plate number. Hard data. Something I could take to the authorities, along with all the rest I knew.

But to read it I'd have to creep around and lean over to

wipe it clean.

That's when it all went wrong. I crept closer to the license plate and felt my foot squish into something soft and wet, like pudding: a plastic bag, I could see, with the outline of a decomposing human being in it—a disintegrating body, slowly turning to liquid.

My head jerked upward! I knocked a metal pot from a shelf! It hit the ground with a loud *clang*!

Dammit!

I started to run. Lights began to come on—illuminating the yard. I heard a door slam. Five men who looked a lot like the television watcher ran from the house. The first three had guns.

I bolted across the brightly lit yard and down the road. I tore down the road as fast as I could, headed for the protection of the thick woods where I'd stashed the bike. I could hear them after me, on foot, and then there was a *boom!*—a shot—just as I reached the protection of the trees.

Suddenly I felt a sharp burning sensation in my left shoulder and reflexively put my hand over my ripped shirt and felt the warm, sticky blood oozing from a fresh wound. I glanced over my shoulder. The men were close behind. I darted to the left, away from the bike. They followed. I kept running, pumping my legs as hard as I could until I reached a ravine. Without breaking stride, I jumped in, changed direction, and doubled back toward the bike.

The Missile Game

Behind me, I could now hear the men shouting at each other in confusion. They'd gone past the ravine and I'd apparently disappeared.

The bike was close-by. I could get on it and escape. I yanked the bike out of the bushes and jumped on and started pedaling down the road. My heart was thumping in my chest by now and I was panting like a triathlete racing for the finish line. I pedaled as hard and as fast as I could, standing on the pedals to get optimal thrust with each rotation.

In the distance, back toward the house, I heard the truck fire up and charge out of the garage. It's wheels squealed as it hit the road and turned in my direction.

I could hear it coming from behind. Just seconds before the truck's headlights illuminated the road, I swerved hard into the woods and darted left and right through the thick stands of trees. I was in the dark and veering around fallen logs and rocks. I was trying to take routes I thought no one could follow. Briars ripped my arms and low-hanging limbs slapped my face.

I could hear the truck turning into the woods. Its lights came on and cast a flying, flashing light through the trees. The men on foot had clearly regrouped and were somehow in coordination with the truck now. I could hear them moving in the forest.

Then I heard it: the sound of a flowing creek. It was the best way.

I raced toward the sounds of the creek. It was my only hope. I found an opening in the trees and flew down the bank and into the water. The flowing creek reached the middle of my wheels but the bike kept moving. Within seconds I'd crossed the water and had dismounted and was now carrying the bike.

I glanced over my shoulder. On the opposite side of the creek, the front end of the truck had come barreling down the slope and was in the water, but its rear end was still up on the bank. I could hear the wheels spinning in the mud. It was stuck.

I came to a path on my right. I hopped on the bike, and hoped it led to a main road. A few minutes later, miraculously, I came out on Emmaus Church Road.

The house was no more than 100 yards away, on the opposite side of the street.

I heard an engine turn over.

Shit! The Caddy!

Hopping off the bike, I ran into the bushes and hid by the side of the road, my head down. The Caddy whizzed by. I waited until it was out of sight, then pedaled as fast as I could, taking country roads and back alleys all the way back to Keyes' apartment.

42

Keyes' Apartment
11:00 p.m.

THE MUSCLES IN MY legs cramped as I unlocked the door to Keyes' apartment. I stood in the doorway, bent over for a full two minutes, then parked the bike in my room and headed straight to the shower. I was sweaty and exhausted from the chase through the woods and the thirty-six-mile round trip to Chapel Hill. I peeled off my shirt and appraised the deep, blood-encrusted, three-inch-long crease in the flesh where the bullet had grazed my upper arm.

Could've been a lot worse, I thought with a shrug.

I dropped my pants and stepped into the small shower enclosure, happy to be alive. With the water as hot as I could take it and lots of soap, I thoroughly cleansed the bullet wound as well as the scratches covering my body.

An hour later I was drinking coffee and pacing the floor, trying to figure out what to do. That was a dead body in that garage. I'd been shot. I had to go to the police. A chill came over me. *Oh, God. "The Killer Doc," that's me. How am I supposed to explain all of this? I'm going back to jail. The minute I open my mouth, I'm "The Killer Doc."*

I was going over my predicament when Keyes returned. I looked out the window to see if anyone had followed her. I saw no one.

She didn't look at me as she sat down next to me in the kitchen.

"Hey," she said flatly. Her hands were shaking, and her voice was hoarse.

I put my hand on her shoulder, and she flinched. "Are you all right?"

She nodded but still didn't look at me. "Yeah, I'm okay. Just tired."

I pretended not to notice the tears brimming in her eyes. She looked down at her hands for a moment, and then at me. "You're still here," she said, forcing her lips into a half-smile. "You're not hanging by a necktie from a ceiling beam."

She then turned her eyes away and walked directly to her bedroom, closing the door behind her. I went in and took her by the arm. She turned to face me.

"You're in danger, aren't you?" I said more than asked.

She looked at me and began to cry.

"Tell me what's going on."

She put her finger to her lips and beckoned me outside

to the stairway. She spoke in a whisper. "Someone bugged my apartment. There's one in my phone and one in each room, in the light fixtures."

I tried hard to keep my voice down. "For God's sake, clue me in. I want to help you!"

Keyes looked me in the eye and then looked away. "Listen, I don't know what's going to happen over the next few days, but … well, there are things in my past that I'm not proud of that might come out. It's very complicated … I need you to always remember that whatever I may have done, I had a good reason to do it."

"Okay," I said. "Is there anything you want to tell me now?"

She looked me in the eyes. "Just that … I'm in as much trouble as you are, maybe even more."

I looked into her eyes for a long time. She was stalling. "Are you Celena?"

"Just remember, no matter what you hear, I'm really one of the good guys."

She was stalling again. I just stared.

"There is a terrorist attack coming in America, Scott. I'm trying to learn when and where the attack will be."

"*You* are."

"Yes."

"Why *you?* Are you Celena?"

She hesitated before saying, "No, Scott. The CIA has

me posing as an undercover courier for ISIS. I delivered that message to Celena, who is ISIS. There's a civilian contractor, code named Alpha Charlie. He operates drones from somewhere in the southeastern United States. He kills targets in Afghanistan and Pakistan and now Iraq and Syria. When Celena finds Charlie, ISIS will send missiles, big ones, to wipe out Charlie and his headquarters. I have to find where ISIS keeps its missiles and report it to the Agency, so they can stop the attack."

I thought for a moment. I wanted to believe her but it just seemed all too unbelievable.

"If you're with the CIA, what are you doing working in my office? *And*, why did you bother helping me?"

She hesitated ... "Because Herb Waters launders money for ISIS—"

"Waters?"

"We *think* he does. We're not sure. We think he makes a lot of his money that way. We believe he may have laundered some money for Al Qaeda at one time. We're tracking him. He may know about the ISIS operation. You've done a lot of research on Waters and his financial dealings. Maybe more than us."

"Thanks, but ... "

She paused. "You're also at war with him."

"How could he possibly launder money for a terrorist organization?"

"Easy. Through the hospitals. He's arranged the finances so that only he knows them. He can move millions through a hospital and then convert it all into innocent-looking payments."

"Who's Celena?"

"Scott, I can't divulge that to you."

A shock went through me. "Hold on. Is Jackson City Hospital in any danger of being bombed?"

It took a moment as she contemplated her answer. "Waters has connections. On both sides. His hospital is safe. Any more questions?"

I shook my head. I knew she was lying. I knew there was something wrong. But still, I wanted to believe her. "Is Anna Duke 'Quasart'?"

"Let's just say that she and I are working together on this. That's all you need to know for now. I'm quitting the CIA job when this is over. My job ends with this mission, and I'll be leaving in two days."

"Who paid my bail? If you're really CIA, you'll know that."

"Let me just say this: I know who paid your bail, okay? I want to help you, Scott, okay? I want to prove your innocence."

I relaxed a little, or maybe I was worn out from all of the trauma. I said, "I've been wondering: Just how, exactly, does a medical office manager know how to resuscitate a person?"

She was very close to me. I could feel the heat from her body. Avoiding the question, she reached up and suddenly kissed me.

I didn't know what to do. It stunned me. I liked it, but …

She looked me in the eyes for a long time before answering, "It's just CPR. It's no big deal. It's a part of the classes I took at St. Mary's. Every person who works in a medical office should know that kind of stuff."

But I was thinking about what she'd done *besides* CPR—administering Narcan, properly using the anesthesia machine, clearing mucous from my throat. Her answer, I knew, was another lie. Bea Jones, my previous office manager, might have known CPR, but she couldn't have done any of the other stuff. I was about to ask more questions, but I knew she hadn't faked the emotions she'd showed me, and I really didn't want to know any more. I leaned over and kissed her. I felt the warmth of her lips. It was so easy to fall in love with her.

And I knew she was lying.

She put her hand behind my neck and prolonged the kiss. Finally, she pulled away and I looked into her eyes. They sparkled.

43

Keyes' Apartment
5:32 a.m.

 I WANTED TO BELIEVE Keyes. I also knew that I had a responsibility to tell the authorities. Clearly, an attack was coming and Keyes was involved somehow.

I got up right after sunrise, dressed, and headed for my office. The mountain bike was basically shot, so I was on foot again.

I immediately called Harris.

About half an hour after I'd called him, there was a knock at the front door of the surgery center. I cautiously peered out the window and saw Detective Harris standing there.

I still wasn't sure about Harris, but I couldn't help myself. I had to tell him everything. I was acutely aware, however, that in his eyes I was still suspected of murder.

A murderer.

I had to explain what I knew without appearing crazy.

Handing him a mug of steaming coffee, I said, as calmly as I could, "I think there are terrorists in the area."

"You're not the only one."

"Pardon me?"

"Some creepy little guy named Simpkins was in my office last week claiming that there were some kind of foreign subversives working in our area. He didn't look legit and we didn't know what the hell to do with him."

I reached into my chest pocket and pulled out the half-shredded business card of Harold Simpkins, and silently handed it to him.

All that came out of his mouth was, "A-*hem* … Okay … "

Then I simply quoted, verbatim, the messages I'd seen in Keyes' room, and her claims that ISIS was planning to attack with missiles, as well as the supposed existence of "Alpha Charlie."

Harris' face seemed frozen. I was scared that I looked like a madman.

Then, though I didn't want to, I told him about my little adventure at the house on Emmaus Church Road, the previous night.

By the time I was done, Harris was sitting on the edge of his chair. The veins in his neck and forehead were bulging. He growled, "I've gotta report this ta the sheriff in Chapel Hill right away," and then stood and walked straight out to his car.

While Harris went to his car and made several calls, I took a moment to look over what was left of my dying orchids. Even dried and uncared for, they were still beautiful to me.

The detective was breathing hard but smiling when he returned. Slapping me on the back, he said, "Good God, Dr. James, I should chew ya' out for snoopin' around on yer own like that! But—wow! You did somethin' *big*."

I thought about what I should do next. When you're accused of murder, you become wary of your own actions. You question everything. You feel like you have to prove something. "I'll confront Keyes myself," I said.

"No! Not yet. For God's sake, just stay cool. Watch her like a hawk and see what you can get her to admit to. I have to alert all the agencies up and down the line. Damn. This is getting bad. First Simpkins, then there were two foreigners seen walking around the hospital Penthouse rooftop a couple a days ago, now this."

That got my attention. I blurted out, "Jackson City Hospital? *The* Penthouse?"

"Yes. Do you have any idea what the hell they might be doin' up there? I woulda' called hospital security or sent a patrol car over, but the way Waters is so crazy, I figured if they were Waters' men, he woulda' thrown a fit."

I wasn't sure what to say, so I changed the subject: "I'm

beginning to like her, frankly. Elizabeth Keyes, I mean."

"Well, maybe this will help ya a bit: Because of the … ahem … recent murders … I called Odessa, Texas, and did some checkin' on Elizabeth Keyes. There's no record of her being born or attending high school in that area, like she claimed on the application she gave ta your office. She did train briefly at St. Mary's, but the rest of her story doesn't check out."

"Here's a question for you, Detective: If she *is* lying, and she and Waters are working with ISIS and—?"

"And planning a terrorist attack?" Harris finished my question.

I shrugged.

"I'm going to call my buddy up at Camp Peary," he said, "who's in touch with the anti-terrorist people in DC. I'll go through him." His voice was thick with tension. "You stay with Keyes." He hesitated, then said what I knew was coming. "Doc, if her story doesn't check out with the CIA, we're going to have to arrest her."

44

4360 Emmaus Church Road
Chapel Hill, North Carolina
11:30 a.m.

 HARRIS' ALERT "UP AND down the line," set in motion Chapel Hill's Sheriff, Jonathan Stone, and three of his patrol cars. They raced to Fordham Road and waited less than five minutes before two cars of the State Police, and a minute later, a SWAT team roaring up in a van, arrived. The cars surrounded the decrepit old house. Stone got all the agencies coordinated with the SWAT team, and then sent them in. They kicked open the front and rear doors simultaneously and moved quickly through every room. The house was vacant. They went to the garage. The Cadillac and Ford truck were not there.

As the SWAT team searched the land around the buildings, Sheriff Stone and the State Patrol Chief explored the house. People had been staying there for several weeks. The food in the trash containers was fresh, probably served last night. The water had been turned off the past six months, and the toilet was overrun with excrement. Piles of human feces were scattered over the property. All the sinks had been used as urinals.

The occupants had made a hurried evacuation during the night. Tire tracks gave evidence that a truck and a car had been parked in the garage. Fingerprints were everywhere, as was DNA material. The state lab in Raleigh came to take evidence in an attempt to identify the persons who'd illegally occupied the residence.

Jackson City Police Station
11:30 a.m.

As soon as he reached his desk, Harris called his friend, Roy Perkins, the Field Operations Commander at Camp Peary. Harris told him about the notes citing a missile strike in America, men on top of the hospital, the discovery of what looked like a safe house, and his weird visit from Simpkins. At last, Harris asked, "What're we supposed to do about all this?"

"Pete, I need you to come out here to the base."

"Oh yeah? Why's that?"

"We need to have a little talk."

Camp Peary, Virgina
2:04 p.m.

Roy Perkins stood only five feet, three inches tall, and was balding, but Pete Harris and others considered him a giant. Perkins lived at the center of the anti-terrorist effort on the east coast of the United Stares. Harris had met him first during a combined-agency Emergency Preparedness exercise that Perkins had hosted at the base for all the law enforcement officials and first-responders in the southeast. Afterward, they'd talked about the finer points of fishing over beers at the officers' club until the place closed up for the night.

When Harris finally arrived at the base, Perkins ushered him into his office and said, without any introduction, "We can't discuss any of this on the phone—if that can be helped."

"No problem at all, Roy. But what the hell is all this? There's something going on around The Jackson City Hospital, and I need to know what it is."

"There's a man in the area. A real hot shot. 'Alpha Charlie' they call him—"

"I'm aware of Mr. Alpha Charlie," Harris groaned.

"He goes to Afghanistan and does contract work with drones. It's rumored that this guy is preparing to do his Iraq and Syria contracts from the States, somewhere near Peary," Perkins said. "It's possible that a foreign cell may be here in The States with specific instructions to take him out."

"So this Keyes individual—"

"We're going to check into her right now. If she's in deep, it may take a little time to find out who—and what— she is." A grave look came over the compact little general's face. "We've heard the code name 'Quasart' before. If a

173

message was indeed sent from Quasart to Keyes, then we simply must use Keyes to find Quasart. Have this doctor guy stick to her like glue, but don't give our position away by bringing him too much into the loop. I'll talk to Surveillance. I'll have her phone tapped."

"Listen, Roy, there's something else I should mention: Two different cops, both of 'em mine—Jackson City guys—over the past two nights—have reported that men in black suits and hoods were behind the hospital, in Mariner's Wood."

"Forested area. Behind the hospital. Yeah, I know of it."

"I'm gonna' go over there tonight."

Perkins had been kicked back in his chair. Now he sat upright. "If there's actually something going on in those woods, you may be in over your head."

"Naw. I don't think it's anything yet. It'll be fine. I'll just watch from a distance."

"Eh … I don't know. Maybe you ought to take a couple of guys. Maybe we need to get some people in at a higher level. We're going to have to talk to the FBI anyway."

"Don't worry about it. If I come up with somethin', I'll phone you right away. Otherwise, I'll buzz ya in the mornin' and give ya my report."

45

Jackson City Hospital
3:30 p.m.

 Herb Waters called an emergency hospital board meeting. For this command performance, all twelve board members were punctual.

"We have a hacker," Waters began. "And the violation came from the hospital website." It was obvious that Waters was about to blow. "Whoever it was hacked into the hospital's board minutes. Apparently, someone's interested in our communications with AHS," Waters said. "On the record, we're not pursuing the sale of the hospital, but our continued dialogue with AHS is getting some attention, especially since Dr. James publicly criticized how we run our hospital. Any mention of AHS in our minutes could be misleading and detrimental to the hospital's best interests."

LeShaun Washington, a board member who also happened to sit on the Jackson City Council, asked, innocently, "Is there potential for a future sale?"

Waters' face flushed, but he quickly recovered and said flatly, "Such considerations are for hospital leadership to decide. This hospital board has no say in the matter."

Waters walked to the coffee pot and deliberately filled his cup very slowly as the directors looked at each other in stunned silence. Then, he returned to the table wearing his best smile and handed out flash drives. "This is a program that will erase any sentence in your computers that mentions AHS."

Chris Johnson, probably the only one on the board with any real curiosity, loosened his tie, then turned and whispered something in Chief Counsel Mark Levinson's ear.

Waters clenched his fists. "Chris, if you have something to say, why not tell it to the entire group?"

Johnson stood. "Well, I was wondering, why is there such secrecy about the contacts with AHS? And why are you reluctant to just tell us what's going on? After all, we are the supervising board of the hospital."

Waters took a deep breath and spoke quietly, "Chris, do you not trust me as the president of this board?"

Johnson opened his mouth to speak, but said nothing.

Waters changed his focus to the other eleven members of the board. "If there are any others who doubt my ability to lead this hospital, now is the time to speak up. I'll be happy to release any of you from your commitment to the board and appoint someone else to fill your slots." He raised his voice. "Someone I can rely on!"

Johnson cringed in his seat. He'd just bought a new lake house and needed the money this appointment paid him. "I'm sorry if my question offended you, Herb. Your leadership abilities are without question. Of course you have my loyalty."

Waters gave him a thin smile and then turned to the others. "Does anyone else have anything to say?"

Two of the board members stated their commitment to serving the community in this manner. Another stood and praised Waters' leadership.

"I'll second that," Washington said.

All nodded their agreement.

Waters shook hands with each of the board members and thanked them for their support. Then he excused himself.

For the next two hours, the twelve smiling board members socialized as they were served and enjoyed a lobster dinner and cocktails.

46

Keyes' Apartment
6:30 p.m.

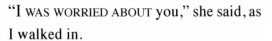

"I WAS WORRIED ABOUT you," she said, as I walked in.

Embracing her in a welcoming hug, I could feel the tension in her body and see it in her face. Anticipating as much, I'd bought a bottle of very cheap wine. "Will you join me for a night cap?"

"I'd love to," she said.

She took off her shoes and curled up on the couch next to me. She raised her glass. "To a good team!"

"To a beautiful partnership," I said, clinking my glass against hers.

I took a long sip, then put my glass on the table and turned to her.

"Thank you. I mean, for everything."

"You're welcome," she said softly, then licked a drop of wine from her lips.

I took her in my arms and kissed her. Initially, she responded with an open mouth, but then she began to

178

tremble and abruptly pulled away.

"I can't. I'm sorry." Her voice wavered and tears filled her eyes as she stood up.

"I'm sorry, too," I said to her as she fled to her bedroom. I heard the door close.

I polished off my wine and hers, and went to bed.

I was lying in the dark staring at the ceiling when the door to the guest room opened and Keyes padded across the floor to the side of the bed.

"Can we talk?" Her voice was soft but strong, no longer wavering.

"Of course." I sat up and turned on the small lamp on the nightstand.

She sat next to me and told me her story. "I never knew my parents. We were a military family. They were killed in an accident on the base. A couple in England adopted me when I was two and changed my name to theirs, Keyes. It wasn't a happy childhood. When I was fourteen, I ran away from that home and started fending for myself in the Bowery of London. I made a lot of money, enough to get out and move back to Texas. So sex for me, well ... "

"Thank you for telling me. I know it must not be easy to talk about. I'm sorry that happened to you."

"Please understand, it's different with you," she said. "As adept as I am at avoiding emotional involvement with men, I have feelings for you I don't understand. I like to

179

tease men and dominate them, but I don't want an emotional commitment to a man now ... or probably ever."

"Okay, I get it."

"Thanks." She sighed, as if relieved.

"We both could use some sleep."

"Goodnight, Scott." Then she kissed me on the cheek and returned to her bedroom, closing and locking the door behind her.

I lay in my bed looking at the ceiling when I heard her open her door, then mine. She came in and closed my door behind her. She stood at the head of my bed for a brief second, and then slowly, confidently, began to strip. She peeled off every stitch until she was naked before me.

"You sure you want to do this?" I asked.

She didn't need to answer. She looked at me like she was going to devour me. My eyes moved slowly over her body. I admired her face, strong cheekbones, soft green eyes, full lips only lightly touched with pale pink lipstick, and wavy blonde hair that bounced on her shoulders.

I stood and approached her. I opened my mouth to speak and was surprised at what I said: "Can I touch you?"

"Yes ... I'd like that."

Elizabeth responded by putting her arms around me and pulling me even closer.

We stayed together in bed all night, embracing, kissing, fondling, and sleeping. I felt happy for the first time since I could remember.

47

Mariner's Wood
Jackson City, North Carolina
1:02 a.m.

HARRIS PARKED AT THE front of the Jackson City Hospital, then began walking from shadow to shadow to the rear of the building, and Mariner's Wood.

Mariner's Wood stood just behind the hospital, separated only by a single, rough road. The lightly forested area had been paved with gravel and was used primarily for overflow parking, and for the storage of the hospital's mobile units.

Four RVs that looked like ambulances on steroids were parked there in the dark. One was used for cancer screenings and a second for mammography. They were deployed on a weekly basis for screenings in the remote areas of the Smokey Mountains and in the smaller coastal towns in eastern North Carolina.

The other two RVs both had "Jackson City Emergency Disaster Hospital" painted on their sides in giant red letters. These were massive mobile units, whales, with treatment areas, laboratories, radiology suites for X-rays, MRIs, and CT scans, a pharmacy, and two small but fully equipped operating rooms. One mobile unit alone had treated 200 burn and trauma victims during a West Virginia coal mine collapse.

The mobile units were empty and dark now, and there were no other vehicles parked in Mariner's Wood. The place was quiet.

Harris maneuvered until he was standing just inside the opening of a narrow tunnel at the back of the hospital, and then waited for two long hours. He grew weary of the fruitless night vigil. People were seeing things. There was nothing out here.

Then something caught his eye—movement in the trees behind the building. He watched attentively for another thirty minutes. Then, a faint glow of light came and went in a fraction of a second. It was a burning cigarette.

With his pistol drawn, Harris quietly left the tunnel entrance and walked to the edge of Mariner's Wood, only fifty feet from the rear of the building. He stood behind a large red oak tree and peeked around. He smelled tobacco smoke. Someone was close.

Suddenly, the tobacco smell intensified and a limb cracked. The person was behind him. Harris aimed his pistol as he turned to face his attacker. In that moment, the palm of a large hand slapped down hard on the top of his head. The extraordinary downward force instantly shattered his spine and compressed the spinal nerves. Sharp pains shot from his back and into his arms and legs, even into his hands and feet. Harris tried to fire his gun but he couldn't pull the trigger. He was paralyzed.

Coarse fingernails dug into his scalp. A heavy, half-round, ten-inch blade sliced his throat to the bone. A second thrust found the space between two vertebrae and cut entirely through the neck. Harris' body fell to the ground.

A black SUV drove slowly into the woods. The driver and the killer threw the body and head into the trunk.

48

Keyes' Apartment
8:05 a.m.

KEYES WAS STILL IN my bed when I awoke the morning after our night of lovemaking. I turned and kissed her. "I'm glad I didn't succeed in knocking myself off. It would've been a shame to miss last night."

Keyes held me tightly and whispered, "I feel good today, better than I have in a long time."

"Me too," I said, stroking her hair from her face

I opened my mouth to speak, but she shushed me with a kiss.

"I'll make breakfast," she said.

As we ate, I looked into her sparkling eyes. They were so inviting.

God knows I needed an ally, so over breakfast, I filled her in on my situation. "I know Waters had a hand in Dr. Carey's and Willie Wilson's murders. He's the only person I can think of who would try to kill me or discredit me," I said. "I wrote that letter to the paper about all the shady stuff that's been going on since he's been running the show at the hospital. Now he's trying to sell it. Somewhere along the way, there has to be something that could expose Waters' dealings."

"Maybe I could find a way," she said.

Thirty minutes later, enough time for me to clean up the breakfast dishes, Keyes walked into the living room wearing form-fitting white jeans and a sheer, ruffled, sky-blue blouse, one that brought out the green in her eyes. Her hair and make-up were flawless, and stunning emerald earrings dangled from her ears. She could've stepped out of an issue of *Vogue*.

"Where are you going?"

"I have to run an errand."

49

Air Harbor Airport
Greensboro, North Carolina
Noon

KEYES QUICKLY CLIMBED THE steps and entered the private Learjet parked adjacent to runway eight.

"I'm so sorry I didn't have time to get more dressed up, Omar," Keyes said as she sat at a round table laden with a lavish spread of foods and wines. She was gorgeous. Her blue blouse ballooned out at the waist, accentuating her breasts. Her blonde hair fell, elegantly, straight to her shoulders.

"Omar, I'm still having some … issues … and need a little more time. Will you please ask Hormand for an extension for me?"

Omar Farok wore a white suit and an open-collared white shirt, expertly tailored to fit his trim, five-foot-eight-inch body. He ignored the question and leaned over the table. He grasped her fingers tightly in his small, oiled, manicured hand. A wide-banded gold ring with a sparkling five-carat blue-white diamond flashed on his ring finger. His long, thin face was smoothly shaven and splashed with sweet-smelling aftershave lotion. His thin lips barely moved as he said quietly, "You, my dear, have always been beautiful, every second of your life since you were born."

"But the deadline—"

"Shh … I want you to have something to enhance your beauty." He looked upward, his eyes catching the gaze of his well-groomed servant wearing a white thobe, with a red and black embroidered waistband.

The servant walked to the table, his outstretched hands holding a shiny object. Farok took the gold and platinum Rolex watch. It was covered with diamonds and emeralds. Looking into her eyes, Farok clasped the watch onto Keyes' wrist. "My dearest, I have loved many women in my life, but you are my most precious gem. I want you to be mine, heart and soul. This gift to you is but a token of my forever love for you. It is important to me that you always wear this symbol of our love and that you promise never to remove it from your arm, whether you are at a party with the Queen or planting flowers in your garden."

She smiled as she touched the treasure he'd given her. As beautiful as it was, her sole objective tonight was to escape a horrible death. Her deadline had expired. She was here to beg for mercy.

Returning his gaze, she said, "Omar, it is gorgeous. I

will never take it off, if that is your wish. But please, give me a few more days to find Alpha Charlie."

Farok looked up as a second servant appeared, lifted a bottle of champagne from the ice, and poured it into their glasses.

Holding his glass high, Farok said, "When you return home, we will have the most elegant wedding ever held in the Sudan, and you will be my wife."

Was a marriage proposal her escape from her death sentence? She tried to smile. After drinking the champagne, Farok took her hand and led her to the bedroom of his Learjet. His eyes never left her face as he undressed and lay down with her.

She cringed at his touch. Her mission tonight was to have Omar intervene and spare her life. Lovemaking was not on her "to do" list.

His hands moved slowly over her body. "Oh, my," he uttered, as his hands caressed her breasts. "I love your breasts. And your face is prettier than ever."

Her body stiffened with Omar's every touch.

"My God," he said as he felt the silky smooth skin of her delicious womanhood. "I love it."

"Please … about Hormand's deadline?"

She asked again, her voice now shaking.

He never responded.

After he'd had her, he lay at her side, breathing heavily.

A smile crossed his usually neutral facial expression. Before he went to sleep, he said again, "Never, never remove my love token from your arm."

She asked again, but he made no comment or concession about her request for an extension of Hormand's deadline. She was trembling as she left the bed and put on her clothes.

What was she going to do now?

50

Jackson City Police Station
9:30 a.m.

KEYES DIDN'T COME BACK that night, and in the morning she still wasn't in the apartment. I walked to the police station to see Harris.

I waited at the door of his office, while busy police personnel and civilians alike paid me no attention. I looked at my watch several times. By 9:30 I was antsy. I had to check in with Harris and update him on the movements of Keyes.

Finally, I gave up on waiting. I looked around to see if anyone was watching, then peered into his office window, cupping my hands to the glass. A partly opened folder on the desk caught my attention. It was labeled "Dr. Scott James."

An officer walked by slowly and put his hand on my shoulder and I jumped.

"What, exactly, are you doing?"

"Harris told me to meet him here in his office. He said he had things to tell me, about the terrorists. That folder on

190

his desk has my name on it. He wanted me to read it. We were investigating a terrorist cell together … ”

“Terrorists? Pete never said anything about terrorists. You're full of shit. Get out of this office!”

“Okay, okay.”

“And don't take anything.”

Another policeman walked over and asked, “Any trouble here?”

“No problems. I was just leaving,” I said as I walked by the policemen with my head raised high.

I felt my pulse. Seventy. I was pleased. I was almost thrown back in jail but I'd remained calm.

51

Scott James Surgery Center
7:31 p.m.

 KEYES HAD DISAPPEARED. I hadn't seen her for over twenty-four hours. Celena's deadline, whatever it was for, was today.

I'd spent the day looking for information about Keyes and about Dr. Carey's murder.

I went to my office. I hadn't paid any of my bills and was pleased that the power company had not yet pulled my power plug.

As I opened the front door, I walked by a few dozen pieces of mail piled just below the slot on the door. After my last episode of reading mail, I had no desire to open any more letters.

I'd previously searched Keyes' empty staff locker, looking for information about her missed ride, Anna Duke. I'd also looked for anything that might need reporting to Harris. Nothing had come up. But I hadn't searched her office, at the front of my suite.

The Missile Game

I spent an hour or so just rummaging through her desk, where I found a black wig in one of the drawers. I looked at the names and numbers of my patients. I read them, hoping to find one that revealed Keyes' personal contacts.

Shortly after dark, as I was still working, I heard a sound at the front door. I peeked out of Keyes' office. A man with a gun in his hand was coming right for her door. He saw me and shouted. He raised his pistol to shoot. He was an African, a big man with a wide, round face and a French accent: "WHERE IS ELIZABETH KEYES?"

I ducked back into Keyes' office just as the gun fired. The sound of the shot exploded in the narrow hallway and blew a hole in the wall.

I locked the door and threw her desk on its side, then shoved it against the door. I heard the man running to me, shouting, "WHERE IS SHE? WHERE IS ELIZABETH KEYES?"

I had no defense. I looked around for a weapon. The only thing I saw were two empty oxygen canisters awaiting refills, a defibrillator just back from maintenance, and a broken IV pole needing a replacement.

The gunman reached the door. I ducked behind the overturned desk as he rapid-fired six times. Four bullets whistled over my head, two of which shot through where I was crouched, but were stopped by the thick desktop. The huge man slammed his shoulder into the door. The flimsy door lock shattered. The desk held firm. I looked for protection. The oxygen tank!

I grabbed the heavy tank, and just as the door broke open, threw it through the window.

The window shattered. The assassin reacted by shooting at the tank and I grabbed the broken IV pole and lunged at him, right as he turned to face me. Two bullets passed within inches of my ear. The makeshift spear smashed through his shirt and into his chest, ramming all the way through.

His knees buckled. He looked at me with glazed eyes. Blood coughed from his mouth, and he fell.

Behind the broken debris came the sounds of someone else running in the hall. I jerked the gun from the dead man. *Dear God, please let there be more bullets in this gun.*

A second man suddenly appeared in the doorway. He saw me and raised his gun to fire. Like any other kid who grew up in my area, I knew how to shoot. I raised the pistol and fired twice, the sounds deafening, *BOOM BOOM ...*

Then the semi-automatic weapon let out a *click*. The clip was empty. But both bullets had been in the chest. He fell backward, dead.

I sat down. I was trembling. Sweat poured from my body. Now I had two more bodies to deal with—two more murders.

If I told this to anyone but Harris, I'd go back to jail for certain. I tried to phone Harris' office but I was so shocked and traumatized that for moment I couldn't punch in the numbers.

Still no Harris. He still hadn't returned.

I thought about how to dispose of the bodies. Drug deals regularly occurred at the East End Apartments, three miles from my office. Four months ago, two men were shot and killed and left in a car there. Those bodies weren't found for three days. Three days would help me a lot.

I slapped on surgical gloves, shoved one of their pistols in my belt, and searched the bodies for ammunition. I found ten clips of ammo.

I bundled the men in sheets, and dragged the bodies to the trunk of their new BMW 7000.

I drove to the East End Apartments and parked in a section where there were no lights or people wandering around. Continentals, Jaguars, and Cadillacs were parked in the complex where drug dealing was common. The BMW was not conspicuous.

I jogged back to Keyes' place, taking the cool air deeply into my lungs and feeling very lucky to be alive.

52

Keyes' Apartment
10:00 p.m.

 SURPRISINGLY, I FELT NO guilt about killing the two men. They had come to kill me, and I did what I had to do in order to survive. The strenuous workout of loading the pair of 200-pound bodies in the trunk of the car, and then jogging all the way back to the apartment, actually raised my spirits.

It certainly stopped my hands from shaking.

I had only one regret: that the men had nothing on them that linked them to whoever was behind all this. Now, after taking a hot shower and drinking some coffee, my mind was clear and my motivation strong to figure out who was trying to kill me and why.

I began making a list of the events that had happened in the last two days, when Keyes, at last, came through the door. She walked in, stopped, looked at me, then walked over to the table where I was writing my list and picked up the pistol I'd taken off my would-be killer.

The Missile Game

She raised the barrel of the pistol and held it two feet from my head. My eyes followed the pistol up Keyes' arm and into her face. Her stare was fixed on me, and the muscles in her jaw stood out. "Who gave you this gun?" she demanded.

"It's mine. I had it in my office. Please don't point that at me."

She kept the pistol aimed at my head. "I never figured you'd own a pistol like this."

"Why?"

"It's a custom-made, Browning BMD, 9-by-19 mm. It had to cost ten grand. This has a fifteen-shot clip, and it was made in 1998, when it took a dealer's license to buy it. Until 2004, only the ten-in-a-clip models were sold to the public. You didn't buy this gun. So, now, you want to tell me how you really got this?"

"Considering the line of work your presently in, I'm not shocked you know that."

According to what she just said, the gunman in my office shot at me thirteen times. Thank God there were fifteen bullets in the clip. The last two shells had taken the second killer's life and saved mine. Avoiding her question, I said, "Someone in my office tried to kill me with it this evening at about seven. He failed. I got the gun. Satisfied?"

"Who tried to kill you?"

"What difference does it make?" I said.

I had been told by Harris to play it cool, but I couldn't help it any more. I turned the heat up on her. I had to have the truth. "I'm not so sure about your CIA story." I paused. "And why don't you tell me about your connection with Waters?"

To my surprise, instead of pressing me for an answer to her question, she answered mine. "He and I were friends— or rather, acquaintances—for two months. That's all."

She turned from me, threw the pistol on the couch, and walked to her bedroom, slamming the door behind her. I looked at the gun with more respect than I previously had.

From down the hall, I heard Keyes begin to cry. I went to her room. The door was closed. I didn't knock; I went straight in. She was lying face-down on her bed, sobbing uncontrollably.

"You okay, Elizabeth?" I said as I sat down on the bed and laid my hand on her shoulder.

She turned over and looked at me through her tears. "That's one of Farok's guns! Omar Farok, the ISIS commander! The bullets in that gun were meant for me. I'm the one they were after. My deadline is over, and it's only a matter of time before I'm dead!"

"Then, you're Celena?"

"Yes. I lied to you." She burst into tears and held me tightly. "I'm not working for the CIA. I work for Omar Farok. Farok is now ISIS. He's the one planning the attack.

The Missile Game

I met him when I worked as a courier in the Middle East. He was the pilot who flew me back and forth between Damascus, Yemen, Kandahar, and Syria. I was paid by Al Qaeda. I even went through two months of military training with them. But I was only a courier, never a soldier. But you have to believe me. I don't want anybody to die. I'm just doing this one thing, and then I'm going to hide in South America."

"You can't just give them information that could cause the deaths of thousands and then just run away."

"I have no choice! They're going to kill me if I don't help them. I have a contract on my head!"

"I don't know what to believe anymore."

"Well, you can believe this: The assassin that came to your office for me, wasn't going to shoot me there. He was going to take me to Omar."

"What does Farok want with you?"

"He likes to watch his bodyguards rape and torture women. They cut a woman to pieces before she dies. They killed my best friend like that last year. And I've heard of others. It's horrible the way they're killed, and I know Omar plans to do that to me. I'm so scared of dying that way. That's why I've done everything he's told me to do. I've tried to escape several times, but you cannot escape from Omar."

She cried as I held her close to me. "What about Waters

and the missiles?" I asked.

"Waters is Alpha Charlie."

"I had a feeling, but still—"

"It's true. He's a highly paid hit man. Omar and his group are going to send Silkworm missiles to destroy his control station when I find it, and I think it's somewhere around the hospital. If I don't find it soon, they'll probably kill me and just bomb the whole town."

"That makes a lot of sense. We use to play video games for days. I'll bet Waters is good with drones. But do you really think the drone controls are in the *hospital*?"

"Yes … No … I don't know. I'm not sure. Maybe we were wrong. If I tell them the controls are in the hospital and they're not, they'll be even harder on me."

"How can you do this? By not going to U.S. authorities, a lot of people will be killed."

"I don't know! I don't want to hurt innocent people, you have to believe me!" she cried. "But if I find the drone control center and report Waters' whereabouts to them, I'll be free! If I don't, they'll be after me for the rest of my life or until they catch me and torture me to death!"

I pulled her into my arms and held her. As we rocked together, I whispered into her ear, "We'll find Alpha Charlie and make things right. And somehow, we'll stop them from firing their missiles. I promise."

"That's why I couldn't tell you this earlier. They'll kill

you, too, just the way they'll kill me. It's so horrible, you can't imagine. It's not like they're directed by ISIS; Farok's men are Congolese and do things like ancient tribesmen did centuries ago. They are known to slice off pieces of victims and eat them while the victim watches. Can you understand why I'm so afraid?"

I sat on the bed and held her tightly. I understood her fear of Farok and her need to save herself. "You kept me from killing myself. Now, it's my turn to save you."

Exhausted, we slept fitfully through the night.

53

Keyes' Apartment
7:41 a.m.

 As we lay in her bed together, Keyes' computer suddenly emitted a short musical alarm. She jumped out of bed and began reading a message on the screen. She turned to me and spoke fast. "To prove to you that I'm telling the truth, read this."

DRONES ARE ACTIVE. PAST HISTORY SAYS HE WILL KILL IN THE NEXT EIGHTEEN HOURS. ACCELERATE YOUR SEARCH. THIS IS YOUR ONE LAST CHANCE OR YOU WILL BE ELIMINATED.

"Is this from Farok?"

"Yes."

"Is he the one who gave you the watch?"

She nodded her head and wiped her eyes. "It was his money that paid your bail."

"You paid my bail? ... Using that pig's filthy money?" She dropped her head and just nodded. "The house in Chapel Hill was yours and Simpkins', right?"

"That was to be my safe house. But the Pakistanis came and set up operations there. Simpkins never actually stayed at the place. Then, Farok rented a farm in Ellsburg for me to set up my computer stuff. I went to the Emmaus Church house once—to instruct Simpkins on where to plant his mics and take photographs. Farok hired him to help me find the drone control."

"Did you ever meet Hormand?"

"Why do you ask?"

"When I was looking through your things, I saw a photograph of an old, balding man in Arabic dress."

She laughed and looked away from me. "Yes. That was Hormand, but I saw him only once, at a party with Omar."

"So how did Waters get involved in all this?"

"Omar learned that Waters was the main drone operator in Afghanistan and Pakistan, and he paid me to get to know more about him. I told you that Waters and I were acquaintances. That was a half-truth. In actuality, as part of my mission for Omar, I dated him a few times. I convinced Waters to get me the job in your office so I could be close to him. He thought it was to date him more, but in reality, it was really just so I could keep an eye on him and locate his drone operation. Since I've been here, I've tried to call him and see him, but he won't even talk to me."

Keyes got up and went to her computer. I sat at her side as she sent an email message to Quasart: "The entire complex explored. No clues found as to location of Charlie or his commend center. I need sonograms of the land around the hospital. Maybe site is underground."

I looked at her and said, "We'll locate Waters' drone control to leverage your release from ISIS. Farok has given you a reprieve of a few hours. That may be just enough."

54

WATERS CALLED SHIRLEY MOSS into his office. As she walked in, he stood and frowned. "I can't locate Detective Harris," he said calmly. "Get him on the line for me."

After ten minutes on the phone, she still didn't have Harris.

Waters screamed, "When I tell you to do something, I expect promptness!" Waters' personal security, the gigantic Michael Jefferson, towered nearby, stone-faced.

"I'm sorry, Mr. Waters, but he's not answering either of his numbers, and no one seems to know where he is."

"Then get his buddy Scott James on the line for me. They have something going on. Harris let him out of jail when I told him to keep him locked up. Call Elizabeth Keyes. She'll know where he is."

James answered after eight rings.

Waters yanked the receiver out of Shirley Moss' hand

and said, in a quiet tone, "Hello, Elizabeth. I need to locate Dr. James."

"Well, so nice to hear from you, Herb."

The veins in Waters' neck and face swelled, and his face became fiery red. "So, you and Keyes are shacking up together. You have her out spying on me, don't you?"

"Herb, you had a chance to have her, but like everything else, you blew it."

"If you fuck with me again, Scott, you'll be sorry. I need to speak to your pal, Pete Harris."

"He's tied up at the moment. Do you wish to leave him a message?"

"When you see Harris, tell him to call me! Right away!" He slammed down the receiver and stood at his secretary's desk.

Shirley looked down at her computer before gritting her teeth and standing. "I always liked Dr. James. What do you have against him?"

Waters suddenly grabbed a half-full cup of lukewarm coffee and threw it at her, striking her chest and splattering lukewarm coffee all over her and her desk. She started to cry and looked away.

He grabbed her shoulders and shook her. "Look at me when I talk to you!"

Coffee dripped from her face as she looked into his dark eyes.

"If you ever betray me like Harris and James have, you'll be out of a job and I'll see to it you never work anywhere in this country again for the rest of your life. Do you understand me?"

"Yes, sir."

Waters returned to his office and kicked the door closed.

Shirley went to the bathroom, washed coffee from her face and tried to remove the coffee stains from her white blouse. She came back to her desk. Her phone rang, but she ignored it. She picked up the coffee-soaked letters she'd typed that morning and threw them in the trash. She started to leave, but turned and went back and opened Waters' door.

Waters looked up. "Where do you think you're going?"

"Home. And I won't be coming back. Ever!"

She slammed the door as she left.

55

The Penthouse
Noon

HERB WATERS WAS IN a rage. Controlling his vast empire put an unfair strain on him, he felt. He needed rest. And sex. He turned on the Skype program, and Elayna appeared nude on the screen.

Elayna performed and then gave Waters a few moments to collect himself, then turned to the screen. "When can I expect you?"

"I have three weeks of work to do. After that, you'll be at the top of my list."

"Make us lots of money, sweetheart. I need some things from Cartier."

Jackson City Hospital
12:31 p.m.

Waters left the suite and entered the Penthouse's private

elevator. He pressed the Express Sub-Basement button, and felt the swift drop. After just a brief moment, the elevator's doors rolled open to reveal the Sub-Basement, a long, dimly-lit tunnel that led away from the hospital. Waters walked swiftly down the narrow corridor, illuminated only briefly by piercing white bulbs. For a brief moment, no one on earth knew where Alpha Charlie was.

Keyes' Apartment
12:33 p.m.

I had to relay all the new information to Harris. Keyes went to take a shower, and I used the opportunity to slip outside to the stairwell.

I dialed Harris' number. The dispatcher said Harris was "on assignment" and not in his office. The detective's mobile phone was off, too, the dispatcher said.

Oh, God. What should I do? What can *I do?*

"But this is extremely important!"

"Yes, we know you think your case is important, Dr. James. I'll tell Detective Harris as soon as he reports in."

A knot formed in my stomach as I sat there feeling helpless, wild thoughts swirling through my mind. I turned off the phone and stood for moment.

Elizabeth Keyes almost pulled the doorknob off the front door of her apartment, swinging it open suddenly and shouting, "Waters is on the move!" Her hair was wet and she was wearing wrinkled clothes that she'd just thrown on. She turned and yelled over her shoulder, "Get your shit together! And bring your Browning pistol and the ten clips!"

My head spinning, I ran to the guest room and threw my stuff and the gun into a small duffel bag.

I ran to Keyes' bedroom. She zipped her suitcase and threw her laptop into a briefcase. I followed close behind as she ran out of the apartment, down the steps, and to her car. She reached into the trunk and grabbed a blue gym bag and put it in the back seat. We jumped in, and she gunned it.

We'd gone only a block when Keyes spotted a black Lincoln Continental. "Duck!" she shouted, as we passed the black car. The Continental pulled onto the street directly behind us. Keyes whipped the Honda onto a side street. She grabbed her cell phone and punched in a number. "Help me," she said into the phone. "Someone's following. Meet me at the parking garage."

Keyes drove fast, dodging through back streets to get to the parking garage beside the Hancock Building. The Continental followed our every turn. "We've definitely got a tail," I said. "I think that may be Waters' man. I don't think it's Farok's hit men."

"Someone was following me yesterday. Probably with the government."

"Jesus!" I said. "The *government*?"

"Just shut the fuck up and duck your head between your legs." She drove to the ground floor of the parking garage and stopped, leaving the motor running. A tall, buxom, black-haired woman ran from the shadows and jumped into the driver's side. Keyes said, "Good luck, Anna," then reached behind and grabbed the gym bag and jumped out of the Honda. She ran behind a nearby car, crouched, then turned and yelled, "Get out, Scott!"

Before jumping out of the car, I looked at the new driver. It was the same woman who had delivered the large cardboard cylinder to Keyes the night before I'd made the calls to Texas. So this was the mysterious Anna Duke.

I ran over to the parked cars and hunched down beside Keyes.

Duke floored it, and just as she roared out the far side of the parking garage, the Continental appeared at the other end and accelerated after her.

Keyes and I quickly and cautiously walked to the second floor. I followed her to a black Toyota Corolla. She knelt down and removed a key from under the car. "Get in," she said.

56

Keyes' Apartment
12:59 p.m.

 ROY PERKINS HADN'T HEARD from Harris in forty-eight hours now. No one had. He decided to use the information that Scott James had given to Harris, and pull the plug. He had to end this thing before it was too late and more people got hurt.

Perkins' people hit Keyes' apartment, picking the lock silently and slipping in unobserved. Obviously Keyes and her new doctor friend had just fled. Perkins' "cleaners" worked the place over. The electronics and the databases would take time to sort out. The documents, most of them having been cross-shredded, could also be sorted out, in time. The cleaners searched every nook and cranny of the apartment, top to bottom.

Rectangular shapes on the dust-covered bedroom floor and bedroom furniture indicated that larger pieces of equipment had been removed from the apartment in the past twenty-four hours. Fingerprints were taken throughout, and sent back to Peary. CIA forensics ran through the worldwide databases and found only James' print matched.

A record of Keyes, on the other hand, could not be found.

The Swan Motel
Jackson City, North Carolina
1:02 p.m.

Piecing together the names and addresses that James had acquired, Perkins could see that he had to keep this thing quiet. He knew where part of the ISIS cell was, but not the location of Quasart, or the missiles that James claimed had to be out there somewhere.

Perkins dispatched two teams to The Swan Motel.

The Pakistani bugging team in the motel room had benefited from Harold Simpkins' nefarious deeds. They'd heard enough to know that they could be discovered at any moment. As soon as they heard the helicopter overhead, they began grabbing their already-packed bags.

Their van was waiting, parked nose out. They flooded out of the motel room and immediately heard faint whooshes from the sky as snipers started picking them off.

A helicopter touched down briefly in the parking lot and two men jumped out. The aircraft took off, and the two from Perkins' team found the key, started the van, and then pulled the bodies aboard and took off.

The aircraft and the van were gone within minutes of the assault.

57

Jackson City
2:59 p.m.

KEYES DROVE AWAY FROM the garage and through the back streets. Her face was red and she was breathing excitedly. "There's no time to waste, Scott. You promised to help me, and now you have to fulfill that promise. I've looked everywhere in the hospital for the drone control center and have tried to follow Waters to it. Even though he stays somewhere in the hospital when he's firing his missiles, I've never been able to find him."

"I don't understand why you need me."

"I've been all over his Penthouse and there's no control station there. I've even placed surveillance cameras all over the hospital and the Penthouse. His drones are flying over Iraq now as we speak. He'll go to his station to fire his missiles sometime today, which means that I'm dead soon if we can't figure this out."

"I still don't know what you want me to do."

"You know the hospital better than anyone, and you know Waters. Maybe you can think of something I've missed."

Looking at her, I saw something I'd never seen before: Panic.

My head was screaming. "I'm not going to help you bomb the hospital."

"There may be another way."

She looked at me.

"Scott, they're going to kill me."

"They're going to kill me, too," I said, "But if there are missiles somewhere waiting to be fired, and if Waters is in the hospital, then a lot of people will be killed in a missile attack on him. I will not be a part of that!"

Suddenly, Keyes' phone signaled a text message. She read it aloud. "Celena: Waters has disappeared."

"Scott, maybe I can kill Waters and deactivate his control center. Maybe that will be enough. Maybe we can find Waters and stop him. If we do that, then maybe they won't launch the missiles."

I pleaded with her. "Let's alert the police. Maybe I can convince them that this is a real terrorist threat."

She made a sharp turn, which threw me against the car door. "Look, Scott, Farok programmed my cell phone for me. If I press "6" and "Send," the missiles are sent. But if I press "8" and "Send" a suicide bomber will come. I never

215

had any intention of dialing six and calling for missiles."

"This is bullshit! These guys want to reap massive destruction on America! They're just like the 9-11 attackers! And they're not going to let you get in their way!" I yelled. "Where are these missiles? We have to stop them! Now!"

I picked up her phone to call the police. "Where are the DAMNED MISSILES?!" I shouted.

Keyes looked at me, eyes wide and mouth open. "I ... I don't know."

"Don't lie to me! WHERE ARE THEY?!"

She shook her head. "They don't tell all their operatives everything. I learned that in the Al Qaeda training. In case someone is captured and tortured, they don't know certain information. But Anna Duke will know."

She punched in a number. Anna answered immediately. "Anna, where are the missiles right now?"

"I can't tell you."

Keyes asked again, begging Anna to tell her the location of the missiles, but Anna held firm. "Don't give me any shit! Just find the target! Now! Or I'll find you and kill you myself!"

Keyes almost rear-ended the car in front of us, swerving around it in the nick of time.

"We have to call the cops," I shouted, "or the CIA, or someone, and get help!"

"You have to help me!" she shouted back.

She reached into the back seat, grabbed the plans of the hospital, and shoved them in my lap. "Where is he? Where could he go?!"

Suddenly I got a better look at the Rolex hidden under the long sleeve of her blouse. It had so many diamonds and sapphires you could barely see the numbers on the face. I thought about the watch. Most Rolexes keep perfect time. Hers was five minutes slow.

We'd been winding our way toward the hospital, and now it came into view. I looked at the big building. What she'd said about me knowing the hospital better than anyone was true. And suddenly I knew where the control center was. It was all very clear. Keyes couldn't find it because it wasn't in the hospital. Not exactly. I just couldn't believe I was going along with all this. It was practically impossible to understand what was going on.

The newest set of drawings in the roll of hospital plans were diagrams for recent rewiring. A variety of lines representing new electrical cables ran across the page. They now ran all the way down the Sub Basement—all the way to Mariner's Wood. "It's in one of the mobile units behind the hospital, near Mariner's Wood. I'll bet it's in one of the Emergency Disaster Units. Waters had one decommissioned about two months ago."

58

Jackson City Hospital
3:00 p.m.

THE MOMENT THAT CAME out of my mouth, we heard gunfire. First, a couple of shots, then a short firefight. It was coming from behind the hospital. I told Keyes to park in Mariner's Wood.

As we pulled up to the woods behind the hospital, a man with an M-16 jumped out into the road in front of us. Keyes stopped to avoid hitting him and rolled down the window. "Bathar! It's me, Celena! Don't shoot!"

The olive-skinned man, no more than twenty years old, with dreadlocks and facial hair stubble, stepped over to the window with his gun pointed at me. The acrid smell of gunpowder gusted into the car. My heart beat fast. The young man was thin, about five foot, eight inches in height, and wore a heavily wrinkled khaki shirt and trousers.

"Bathar, this is Dr. James. He's one of us. Tell our men to protect him."

He pointed to five men hiding in the shadows of the hospital maintenance building. All were small, thin, bare-headed, and clad in khaki shirts and trousers. "Your soldiers," Bathar said, nodding at the men. "We were just attacked. Men in blue jumpsuits. Heavily armed."

Speaking in Arabic, Keyes gave Bathar instructions. I didn't know what to do. I just kept my mouth shut.

A barely audible gunshot came from the direction of the hospital. Bathar suddenly dropped to the ground. Half his head was blown away. We could see men running from the hospital. They were big guys, muscular, like football linemen, each weighing more than 200 pounds, dressed in navy blue cotton coveralls, the uniform of the Jackson City Hospital maintenance workers. "Those are Waters' men," I said.

One of Keyes' soldiers started firing his M-16.

In the distance, we heard sirens.

They'll never make it in time. I don't care if I end up looking like a terrorist. I have to stop this.

Keyes seemed unfazed. She texted a quick message: TARGET IS EMERGENCY DISASTER BUS BEHIND HOSPITAL. ALPHA CHARLIE'S LOCATION UNKNOWN.

She reached back and pulled out a Ruger .38 from her gym bag. Turning to me, she said, "Take out your gun and cover my back."

I snapped a clip in the Browning. I hoped I could handle what was about to happen.

Keyes and her men ran for the Emergency Disaster Unit. I followed with my pistol.

Two more of Waters' men suddenly stepped out from behind the bus. Their loud automatic weapons cut down the first of Keyes' soldiers. Keyes dropped to one knee and fired the Ruger .38 twice. Both men fell. Keyes didn't flinch.

One of Keyes' men was dragging a four-foot section of heavy pipe with welded handles, filled with fifty pounds of lead. Another soldier came up from behind him, grabbed one of the handles, and together they slammed the battering ram into the door of the bus. The aluminum door collapsed and the ram went sailing into the trailer.

Keyes and her men ran inside and there was a sharp firefight. Gun smoke drifted out of the RV's door. Waters' man inside and the two with the ram were dead.

Suddenly shots came from the woods.

As Keyes stepped out the door, a man in a blue jumpsuit popped out of nowhere and pointed his gun at her back. Reflexively, I raised my pistol and shot. The man fell dead.

It was that easy.

"You didn't mention I'd have to kill people," I said.

"Musta' slipped my mind."

More shots came from the woods. Machine gun fire strafed the RVs and killed the last two of Keyes' "soldiers."

Then, from the exit behind the hospital, I saw a tall muscular man with a ponytail emerge. He was carrying an M-79 grenade launcher.

It was Brightman.

But whose side is he on?

My question was answered when Brightman launched a series of grenades at the shooters in the woods. There were four *carumps* as the grenades exploded, and the shooting ceased.

Brightman barked out, "Got'em, Celena."

Brightman ran toward the Emergency Disaster bus. A man in a blue jumpsuit appeared at the far side of the buses and shot. Blood trickled from Brightman's head. He staggered backward and fell just outside the door. Blood slowly leaked into his blonde hair as he lay motionless.

Keyes swiftly spread her feet, crouched, and seeing the bulges of a Kevlar bulletproof vest inside the shooter's jumpsuit, delivered a thunderous shot straight into his neck. The man keeled over.

I looked at Brightman. "I hope he isn't the bomber who was supposed to wipe out Waters."

"No. When I give the signal from my cell, someone else will come with a car full of explosives."

59

Drone Control Center
3:04 p.m.

 WATERS SAT IN THE rear of the Emergency Disaster Unit, working his controls. His eyes remained fixed on the three, twenty-five-inch screens in front of him. He never looked away.

Keyes approached slowly, pointing her gun at Waters, who was sitting on the other side of a large pane of glass. I followed. The smell of gunpowder was intense. Waters was so focused on the monitor he barely even noticed her. Suddenly, Keyes raised her pistol and fired five shots at Waters.

Waters did not fall. Instead, he laughed and pointed at the glass. "State of the art bulletproof glass, my dear. Very thin, but still effective. You're going to have to do better than that to get me."

Keyes reached into her pocket for her phone to alert Quasart and Farok that she'd found Waters and the control center. She had only to press "8" and "Send" to have the ISIS bomber sent.

Suddenly there was motion to the right. Keyes turned quickly. A trap door in the floor sprang open and a large, muscular man—Jefferson, Waters' security man—appeared out of nowhere and slapped her gun away. He grabbed her from behind and held her so tightly that she struggled to breathe. She grunted as her phone fell to the floor. I recognized Jefferson and pointed my pistol, but he used Keyes as a shield.

I could see through the door in the floor that there was a passageway to the Sub-Basement, the secret entrance to the hospital that Keyes and the rest had been unable to locate.

I was shaking and unsure of what to do next. I had my Browning on Jefferson, but didn't have a shot.

"Drop it," Jefferson said, ducking his head behind Keyes' head.

I pressed my finger on the trigger, but hesitated. This was a man I'd talked with many times when I'd gone to Waters' office. He wasn't just an anonymous enemy. He was a man I knew and had once called my friend.

"Drop it! Or I'll kill her!" Jefferson demanded.

I kept my finger on the trigger for a moment, but then dropped the gun.

"Excellent job, Jefferson." Waters said. "The doctor's no threat without a gun. He belongs to me. I want him to watch my gaming skills and see how I made my fortune for a few minutes before he dies. Then, after I'm done here, I want the pleasure of pulling the trigger on him."

"The authorities are on their way," I said. "Game over, Alpha Charlie."

"Ha! You're going to be just another part of your own massacre by the time they get here. So glad you could join us here, Dr. James."

"I've been in contact with Pete Harris."

Waters continued his focus on the target screen, but laughed as though I were a naive child. "Scott, this is just like the video games we used to play. Look at the upper-right screen. That's a video replay of the incident that got me this job."

The black-and-white image showed a deuce-and-a-half-ton truck driving in the middle of an American convoy along a road near Kirkuk. Suddenly, a huge explosion completely destroyed the truck.

"This happened three hours ago. The bomb was an IED planted in the gravel road by ISIS. The American military truck was carrying General Harold Bushey and twelve of his men. Bushey is, or I should say was, the command officer of the Third Infantry Division."

Keyes squirmed and kicked in Jefferson's grasp. She *had* to press "8" and "Send."

Ignoring her, Waters continued. "Today, my Reaper is

armed with four Hellfire missiles. A hit gets me a check for $30 million, immediately deposited into a foreign bank, and I'll never be taxed on a penny."

Waters manipulated the hand controls and placed a computer "square" on the bomb factory that had made the IED that killed General Bushey. An X appeared on the screen. Waters moved it to overlap the square on the target. A quick thrust of his thumb, and a Hellfire entered the screen. A couple seconds later, it exploded. As the smoke cleared, I could see the building was totally flattened.

Waters put his controls on the table and sent an e-mail: Mission complete.

Waters pushed open a bulletproof glass door and faced me. Smiling, he said, "So, Dr. James, before I kill you, I'd like to know, have you been enjoying my old girlfriend?"

Refusing to take his bait, I instead shook my head. "What happened to you, Herb?"

Waters laughed. "The hospital's just a sideline for me, a front, a triviality. I assume you've already figured out that I am selling it."

As long as I kept him talking, I could stay alive, so I answered, "Yeah, but it's such a money-maker for you. Why sell?"

"It's chump change compared to what I'm making with my drones. Within a year, I'll make another couple of hundred million, retire, and play with my drones full time.

And—I've never really enjoyed hospital work."

"Really? Who knew?"

"I've come to see that the rules that apply to most people don't apply to me."

I looked around for a way to escape.

Waters had his henchmen kill Barnes, Jolly, and probably Dr. Carey and Willie Wilson, too. Keyes and I are his next victims. But I can outsmart him. He wants to brag on himself. I'll just keep him talking until I find a way to overpower him.

"Are you delusional or what?" I goaded him.

"For example, I have an extraordinary libido, and my wife is a true nymphomaniac. We each have a villa in the Mediterranean. We have an agreement that we each take on a new lover every two months. Actually, she takes two or three young guys and generally swaps them after a month or so."

"So you got horny and brought Keyes here to seduce her yourself."

"I don't believe in romantic involvement with employees. Besides, I wanted her planted firmly in *your* office. I didn't care about her involvement with Farok at that time. I knew having access to an operative like Elizabeth would give me the chance to discredit you. Get rid of all the stories in town about the great, kind Dr. James."

"Jefferson, Farok is going to bomb this hospital!" Keyes pleaded. "I need to make a call to stop him!"

"Tell that story to the chief, sister."

60

Drone Control Center
3:06 p.m.

KEYES BROKE FREE FOR a split second and jumped for the phone. Waters saw her trick. He grabbed it from her. "So, my dear, is this phone your detonator for a bomb you've planted?"

Waters looked at the contact numbers on the cell phone. "Ah! And these will be your detonation codes, isn't that right, Elizabeth? Well, I'll have to press them all when I leave you people to do my errands. What a pity. ISIS will get all the credit."

I suddenly went at Jefferson with the only thing I had, my fist. My shot to his chin was solid, but it didn't hurt him at all. He slapped my face, nearly knocking me down.

Then he pointed his gun at my head.

"Go ahead! Shoot me!"

He looked like he was about to pull the trigger, but then he said quietly, "Mr. Waters wants you alive. At least for now."

Waters held my gun on me while Jefferson tied my hands behind my back with a plastic zip-tie.

Waters seemed to notice the brilliant, blue-white diamonds in Keyes' Rolex. He walked over and looked at the watch. "That's very nice. Which of your boyfriends gave that to you?"

"A very rich one."

"Yes. Omar Farok is almost as rich as I, and I admire his taste in jeweled watches."

Waters returned his attention to me. "I should kill you both right now, but I can't resist giving you one final demonstration."

I sighed in relief. I had a few more minutes to whip them. I just needed something sharp to cut the plastic hand restraint.

Waters opened the bulletproof glass door, and gestured to the controls. "Dr. James knows what these are."

"Video games."

Waters shook his head. "No. These aren't games, and I don't play. This is the operational brain for the deadliest drones the world has ever seen. My control chair operates them all."

Jefferson interrupted. "Kill them now, boss! Before the cops get here!"

"Be patient, Jefferson. It's entertaining to play with

mice before you destroy them."

I studied the controls, the joysticks, the animated screen.

"They're all mine. The drones. They're the world's finest; I paid more than thirty million apiece for them. This hobby is more expensive than the horses I used to own. But unlike the horses, they yield a real return rather than a capital write-off. The CIA marks the targets, and I eliminate them—for a price, of course. In the last six months, I've made thirty kills. Today, I have another job, and then I will take care of my unfinished business."

A flashing orange light appeared on the board. Waters went to the controls. "Watch how the master does it. Here's my last target for the day."

I watched every move Waters made and the corresponding response on the monitor. It was déjà vu: I saw myself at the video arcade with Herb Waters, flying planes with control panels that looked remarkably like this one. Even the target sights were like those on the fifty-caliber machine guns on the arcade planes. At one time I was better than Waters. But not anymore. I was out of practice and Waters had been honing his skills for years.

Waters stared at the screen. "Abu Al Baghdadi is hiding there in that truck. He's third in command in ISIS. The people who pay my bounty made the decision. My job is to carry it out. I kill; I get twenty million bucks."

Taking advantage of Waters' attention on the drone, I

began cutting the plastic tie on a jagged corner of aluminum where the wall had been shot up.

Waters used a mouse pad to move the cameras on the nose cone of the Reaper drone. A dozen still pictures showed on the monitor. One pictured Al Baghdadi.

Waters fired a missile. As the smoke cleared, the badly ripped truck appeared on the screen, engulfed in flames.

"I just made twenty mil taking out Al Baghdadi. And you and your little girlfriend here are next!" he said, shoving my gun in my face, pressing it on my cheek. "I've looked forward to this since we were kids. I'm going to make you suffer before I kill you. I want the satisfaction of beating you to a pulp and then putting a bullet in your fucking head.

"People used to look up to you and paid no attention to me," he ranted. "But *I* was the one who opened holes in the line so you could run through. *I* was the hero of all those games! But the papers never mentioned that; they just lauded the farmer's kid who ran through *my* holes in the line.

"But all that's changed. The paper, the town, the stockholders—they all adore me now. I'll shoot you and your whore, the disgraced killer plastic surgeon and his accomplice. First, though, I'll bash in your face. In self-defense, of course."

61

Drone Control Center
3:10 p.m.

I HAD TO KEEP him talking. I *had* to. "I have a couple of questions ... "

"Fuck you! I don't have to answer any of your goddamn questions."

Waters' face turned red and he bared his teeth as he shook my pistol in my face.

"Herb, at least tell me what you think of my Browning."

Waters gathered his composure. He paused for a second, realizing he hadn't actually looked at the gun since picking it up from the floor. He took that opportunity now. "Nice. Very nice. I'll do you the honor of killing you with this exceptional handgun."

He chambered a fresh shell, purely for affect, and put the gun to my head.

"What about Harris?" I asked, trying to buy time. "He'll put you in jail for murder, in addition to all your other crimes."

Waters lowered the gun and laughed out loud. "You fool.

You're in over your head. Don't you know Harris is dead? Actually, I sent Jefferson to kill him, but somebody else got him before he had a chance. Jefferson saw them carrying his headless body. Now, without you two to question the hospital sale, I can be rid of this place in a matter of months."

My knees nearly collapsed at the news of Harris being decapitated.

Farok's assassins must have got him.

I looked at Keyes. Tears were in her eyes. She knew how savage they were.

I took a deep breath and said to Waters, "Before you can sell the hospital, you'll have to expose the changes that transferred hospital ownership to you."

"Why? There's no grand announcement to be made, Scott. Some minor alterations appeared in the charter over a ten-year period, nothing all at once. It's all legal and will endure court scrutiny."

Waters put the gun to my temple. I quickly made a statement I couldn't substantiate but tested on a hunch. "Herb, I know you ordered the killing of Cabot Barnes and Quinton Jolly to shut them up. I know you had Dr. Carey killed—and that young cop at my office, too—in order to frame me. I'm the only one who'll stand up to you. You're so damned insecure. You always were. I also know that you're helping Al Qaeda launder money, and now maybe ISIS, too. You're playing both sides to build your little empire. You're going to be exposed as a traitor."

Waters' face turned red. He shook the gun in my face. "You're lying! You don't know any of that shit!"

"Who injected Valium into Dr. Carey's neck? Was it Brightman? That's my guess."

"Right man, Dr. James, wrong drug. He hit him with succinyl-choline, a drug that can't be discovered and is deadly. But I knew about your stash of Valium. Brightman even carried a bag of hospital Valium that he poured in the cabinet with your stock. And you acted guilty by trying to hide it all. You spilled a little, but Brightman threw a couple handfuls more on the floor after you left."

He motioned to Jefferson, who held me upright. Waters smashed me with his fist, punching my face, abdomen, and groin. I absorbed the blows and spat blood on Waters. Waters picked up a three-foot section of a broken, half-inch water pipe, and approached to beat me further. Using Jefferson behind me for support, I arched my back and kicked with both feet. Waters went sprawling against the wall. He lay there, stunned.

Keyes kept looking at her phone.

Waters shook his head, calmed himself, then stood. All the stalling had given me just enough time to work through the plastic bands on my wrists. They were just about to go. I gave a hard twist of the wrists, broke free from Jefferson, and punched Waters as hard as I could. He fell back, badly dazed by the blow. Keyes grabbed for her phone. Jefferson slapped it from her. With all the strength I could muster, I lifted the battering ram from the floor and slammed it into Jefferson's chest. It knocked him against the wall. He shook himself and smashed his huge fist into my shoulder. I fell to the floor on top of Keyes.

Jefferson grabbed me by the collar and lifted me until my head touched the ceiling. The ceiling was constructed of slip-in panels of aluminum. The edges looked sharp. As Jefferson stepped back to throw me into the wall, I yanked out a metal panel and swung it wildly, slashing Jefferson's arm.

Bulky muscle pushed through the six-inch cut in the tight skin covering his arm. He tried to throw me against the wall, but, weakened by the deep cut, there was not enough force in his arm.

I fell to the floor.

Enraged, Jefferson screamed, "Enough of this. Now you die!" And went for the kill.

He raised his foot to stomp on me, but I rolled to the side and the foot crashed to the floor. I reached for the pipe Waters had dropped and slammed it into Jefferson's ankle. A jagged edge, protruding from the pipe, cut deeply into his leg. For the first time in the fight, he screamed and his face twisted in pain.

Jefferson hopped on one foot and then fell to the floor.

62

Watson Farm
Chapel Hill, North Carolina
3:10 p.m.

MICHELLE PACED THE FLOOR of the barn, continually looking at her watch. She kept the launch control remote in her hand. Thirty minutes earlier, Celena had informed her that the control center had been discovered, but she still hadn't confirmed that Alpha Charlie was at the site. Things were in a holding pattern.

60,000 Feet above the Virginia-North Carolina Border
3:11 pm

Omar Farok was visibly agitated as his Learjet 60 flew over the vast Dismal Swamp on the Virginia-North Carolina border. The muscles in his jaw worked and sweat beaded on his forehead.

He called Quasart. "Celena must be with Waters at the drone control center. Use the bomber now and blow it up. Launch the first missile to strike one minute after the bomber detonates."

"But why do we need the missile if the bomber is—"

"In case the bomber fails, we will still achieve our objective."

"You want to kill Celena along with Alpha Charlie?"

"Yes! Kill them both!"

"But I thought you and Celena—"

"I said, send the bomber! And the missile! Now!" Farok bellowed.

"Yes, sir."

Watson Farm
Chapel Hill, North Carolina
3:17 p.m.

Quasart texted Farok: BOMBER ON THE WAY TO CELENA'S LOCATION. ARRIVAL IS 3:37 pm. MISSILE TO LAUNCH AT 3:36 pm for 3:38 STRIKE.

63

Drone Control Center

 BRIGHTMAN SHOOK HIS HEAD and opened his eyes. As he slowly sat up, he brushed away blood from a bullet wound that had creased his scalp and knocked him out. He stood and shook his head. He was still dazed, but sensed Celena was in danger and entered the RV.

"Zahar! Help me!" Keyes screamed when she saw him. "Get my phone! It's in Waters' hand."

Joshua Zahar Brightman stepped toward Waters.

Waters called out, weakly, "Zahar, I pay your salary, not Celena. Kill her. And the doctor!"

Brightman paused. Waters had paid him well for eliminating Carey, Fowler, Jolly, and Barnes. But now Farok was his boss, and Farok paid ten times what Waters did. As Brightman lurched for the phone, something slammed his kidney. Zahar turned to face Jefferson.

For a brief moment, the two giants stood face to face, their heads nearly touching the ceiling. Then Jefferson threw a body block. The entire Emergency Disaster Unit reacted by rolling with the huge men. Brightman raised both arms and threw the huge football player back to the other side. The mobile hospital lurched back with them. I fell to the ground.

Jefferson was not fazed. Ignoring his badly injured ankle, Jefferson locked arms with Brightman, spun around, and yanked the huge blond back across the RV. The entire Mobile Hospital squealed under the strain. The room rolled and equipment flew into the air, crashing all around.

Suddenly Brightman saw an opportunity and smashed his fist into Jefferson's throat. Jefferson had been hit a thousand times in the neck by eager young football players, both his teammates who wanted his spot on the roster, and opponents who wanted to kill him. It was a move to fracture the trachea and permanently disable the opponent. Jefferson had spent hours in the gym developing his neck muscles to sustain such blows, and now he blocked Brightman's punch and grabbed one of his arms.

Brightman tried to put Jefferson in a headlock. Jefferson let go of Brightman's arm and grabbed his leg. He yanked up on the leg and forced the pony-tailed giant to fall backwards, sending him crashing to the floor.

Brightman immediately sprung back to his feet.

Jefferson threw a crushing blow to Brightman's face, splattering blood into his eyes. Brightman didn't even stagger before returning the blow. The two goliaths traded lethal blows to the head, but neither showed any signs of injury. Brightman faked a strike to the face and then pummeled Jefferson's ribs. Breaking bones snapped loudly as Jefferson fell against the wall.

Homing in on the point of weakness, Brightman hammered the fractured ribs. Blood flowed from Jefferson's mouth as he fell to his knees. Brightman continued to hit the defenseless man with smashing blows to the body until Jefferson fell, face forward, to the floor.

Then Brightman turned and started coming at me.

"No, Zahar!" Keyes screamed.

Brightman didn't hear her. He was like a beast on a hunt.

As he raised his fist to strike me, Waters slapped Keyes and she fell backward. The giant turned to help her, giving me time to pick up the battering ram.

I'd seen enough of Brightman, as had my dead, cremated friend, Andy Fowler.

I took the heavy pipe and slammed it into Brightman's body. He didn't fall backward, like Jefferson did. Instead the giant pushed away the fifty-pound weapon and came at me again.

I swung the battering ram as hard as I could, this time centering the strike on the solar plexus. Brightman doubled over in pain from the direct hit to the bundles of nerves in his mid-chest.

The blow knocked the wind out of him.

In Brightman's momentary incapacitation, I gathered every ounce of strength I could muster and swung the ram upward, slamming it into his chin. The force of the explosive uppercut knocked the giant backward and onto the floor with a crash. He blinked several times. Blood poured from his mouth and into his lungs each time he gasped for air. He started turning purple, suffocating from his own blood.

<u>64</u>

Drone Control Center
3:30 p.m.

 I FELT THE BROWNING press to my head. "Dr. James. You're a dead man. With the two of you gone, I'll have no more enemies left in the world."

Waters held the gun perfectly against my head while he stared at Keyes.

"You'll get the death penalty for shooting us."

"I was never here."

Waters pressed the pistol harder against my head and said to Keyes, "Reach into my desk and get my handcuffs, won't you, my dear?"

Keyes brought out the handcuffs and Waters said, "Put them on, both of you."

Waters motioned me forward to join her.

Keyes and I were now chained to the wall railing.

A small speaker at Waters station squawked: "Alpha Charlie, do you read me? This is Edwards. I need you right now! Where are you?"

Turning to me, Waters said, "James, it's your lucky day. Edwards just gave you a ninety-second reprieve, but I'll be right back."

Waters went to his control chair and faced Edwards in the monitor. "I'm here," he said as he placed the Browning to his side and activated the computer system. "What's our status? Is there another target?"

"Affirmative. There's a suicide bomber coming for you."

65

Drone Control Center
3:32 p.m.

"HOW DO YOU KNOW that?"

"The intelligence people at Camp Peary. They've intercepted two messages from a terrorist group near you. One confirms that a vehicle driving toward you is a suicide bomber. The other message says there's also some sort of missile scheduled to launch. We're betting you're the target."

"Understood."

"We have your Predator from Peary airborne at this time. The DE Laser is ready. This'll be a good test for you. You can kill that bomber. He's only three miles away." Edwards said. "Hold on ... I've got another message."

Waters went to the fuse box behind the computer and flipped off all electrical power to the RV. With the heavily tinted windows, the bus was dark, barely lit by a battery-operated lantern.

Red and blue lights flashed in the windows. The police

had clearly taken up a position nearby, but it was impossible to tell where, or how far away.

I said to Keyes, "Sounds like even if the suicide bomber doesn't get us, the missile will."

"I'm sorry, Scott. Farok betrayed me."

Waters ran to the door.

I called out, "You can't just leave us."

"Why not? It's the perfect time. To the police I'm just another frightened soul, evacuating the area. The whole, beautiful, 'missile game' will take care of everything else. I won't even have to dirty my hands with your blood."

"But what about all the innocent people in the hospital? There are over a thousand people in there! Patients and nurses and doctors! People you've known and worked with for years. And think of all the workers and volunteers and visitors. Let us die, if you must, but save them!"

"And blow my cover? No way. Let the hospital be leveled to the ground! Then maybe I'll collect the insurance money and federal government disaster money as well. I'll double my fortune. And all those poor 'innocent people'— well, surely you've heard of 'collateral damage,' Scott."

He turned to the door and called over his shoulder, "Say 'Hi' to that missile for me."

"Please, Herb, let us go!" Keyes shrieked.

"Let your lover, Farok, free you."

He grabbed the knob.

"WAIT! ... Aren't you forgetting something? The Rolex Farok gave Elizabeth. It's probably worth half a million dollars."

Waters stopped in his tracks. He turned around and walked over to Keyes. Grabbing and twisting her arm, he took a minute to admire the jewel-studded watch: ten, flawless, three-carat diamonds on the bracelet band, a multitude of two-carat emeralds on the face of the watch, covered all over with one-carat diamonds and emeralds. Waters knew real precious gemstones when he saw them. "I'm going to rub this in Farok's ugly face someday," he said.

He jerked the watch from Keyes arm and ran to his Aston Martin.

<u>66</u>

Drone Control Center
3:35 p.m.

 I RIPPED A SIX-INCH piece of wire from the wall panel attachment. Handing it to Keyes, I said, "Here, I believe you do this sort of thing in your line of work. Unlock the cuffs."

Keyes didn't blink. She looked over the wire for a moment, then bent it carefully and precisely and inserted it into the slot. The lock released, and off slid the cuff from my wrist.

The moment she'd freed herself, she yelled, "The bomber and missile will be here any minute!"

"Not if I can help it."

I flipped on the electricity to the bus.

"What are you doing? We have to get out of here! Now!"

My mind flashed on the casualties and damage the weapons aimed at the hospital could do. Despite Keyes' contention that Farok was bombing only the drone control center, I suspected that the combination of his suicide bomber and his missile would be enough to wipe out the whole hospital. The few lives I'd altered in my medical career were like a grain of sand compared to the lives that would be lost and the people who would be maimed within minutes, if I didn't do something.

Turning to Keyes, I said, "You go. Save yourself, but I need to stay and do this."

"I'm not leaving without you."

"I'm not going until I try one last thing."

Power returned at precisely 3:35 pm.

Edwards' voice boomed through the BAMUS monitor: "Alpha Charlie! Alpha Charlie! The suicide bomber is only a mile from the hospital! He'll be there in less than three minutes! Where are you? Please respond!"

I went to the control chair. "Colonel Edwards, you're too late. Charlie made a getaway. He's not the good guy you thought. It's a long story; I'll tell you about it someday. Right now, we've got more important things to do."

Edwards jaw dropped open. "Get the hell out of there!"

"No. I'm going to take out the suicide bomber myself or die trying."

"Hold on a damn minute!" Edwards bellowed. "Who the hell are you?"

67

Drone Control Center
3:36 p.m.

"I'M DR. SCOTT JAMES. I'm a plastic surgeon."

"What the *fuck*? I don't need a fucking boob job! There are two tons of TATP in that car, enough to blow up that whole hospital!"

The power of the bombs only strengthened my resolve.

"I know, and I'm going to stop that son of a bitch," I said. "I watched Waters operate this, and I can do it. I know the terrain around here like the back of my hand and I bet I can pick off your bomber."

Edwards muttered, "No way. I can't have an untrained operator—"

"Let me do it!"

"You sure you can really do this?"

I turned to Keyes. "Leave now, just in case I miss my shot."

Tears came to her eyes. "No. If you die, I want to die with you. Besides, you may need me."

The Missile Game

"*Go!*" I yelled. "It's too risky."

"Shut up and do this."

On the monitor, the system was tracking a speeding car. I zoomed in to get a closer look at the car: a gold Cadillac Seville, its rear-end almost dragging on the ground as if something very heavy was in the back seat and trunk. I zoomed in for a close-up of the driver: a middle-aged woman with long, black hair and dressed in a maroon thobe, trimmed in gold, with a green breast plate. Despite a maroon scarf draped around her face and pinned at the neck with an ivory clasp, her face was readily recognizable.

"Anna Duke," I whispered.

"I'm absolutely certain that's a suicide bomber," Edwards said. "I see this all the time in Afghanistan and Iraq. The back of that big Caddy is almost touching the ground. Can you see the sacks of TATP in the back seat? Several thousand pounds of it. And the mason jars with grenades lying on top of the TATP? They're detonators. The glass breaks with any collision, and the handles of the grenades fly off."

Edwards turned from the screen for a moment and then came back. "That's not only a suicide bomber. That's Nicole Banzar, a terrorist on the international most-wanted list for the bombings in London and Madrid. Her code name is 'Quasart'"

"Oh my God. Anna is Nicole Banzar?" Keyes said.

249

"Farok sent her to kill me. I know about TATP. Two tons of it will level the entire hospital and a good part of Jackson City. I never wanted that. Scott, you have to kill her."

One of the monitors showed an aerial map of the hospital campus. The car was approaching from the south.

"You've got about one minute before Quasart reaches the hospital." Edwards shouted.

68

Drone Control Center
3:37 p.m.

"WHAT IS THE DRONE armed with?" I asked Edwards.

"A fully charged DE Laser gun, with enough power for eight shots."

I put my total concentration on the job at hand.

Edwards was standing on his chair, getting as close to the monitors as he could. He looked at his watch. "Damn it, Doc, hurry!"

Taking a deep breath, I moved the X over the target.

Pumping both fists, Edwards bellowed, "That's it! You're on it! Now fire!"

"No, I'm moving too fast!"

I pushed the cross behind the car and touched the trigger lightly. The first beam struck twenty yards behind the target. "The controls are making allowance for the speed differential."

"Damn it, James, I told you—that's a DE Laser! It

moves at the speed of light! You have to put the X directly on the car and fire!" Edwards beat on his chair as he yelled. "Aim and fire again! Now!"

<u>69</u>

Hospital Way
Jackson City, North Carolina
3:37 p.m.

As NICOLE BANZAR DROVE the gold Cadillac Seville toward the hospital, she could hear the sirens.

She pressed the gas pedal to the floorboard. She could see the hospital and the Emergency Disaster bus behind it. Her destiny with Allah was before her eyes! She was just seconds from attaining the greatest feat of her life. She heard the voice of her great God, calling her home. Her turn had finally come. Now, she would give her life to Allah. His faithful servant was on her way to Heaven.

Suddenly a blinding light lit up her rearview mirror. She could see the six-inch ball of brilliant white and orange flame hover over her. "Allah is here! He will save me!" she said aloud.

A split second after that she felt the heat, as her body was totally incinerated. The steering wheel turned to jelly as Banzar's hands vaporized. The vinyl seats melted, the electrical wiring liquefied, and the entire car glowed. The gas in the tank and in all six cylinders boiled for a fraction of a second before exploding all at once and detonating the two tons of TATP.

<u>70</u>

Drone Control Center
3:37 p.m.

 Everyone in and around the hospital heard the gigantic explosion.

Keyes screamed, "Oh my God!" She suddenly started jumping up and down. "Oh my God, Scott! You killed her!"

Edwards appeared on the screen. His uniform was wet with sweat. He shook his head. "That was too fucking close for comfort."

Our reverie in taking out Quasart was brief.

"Don't start celebrating yet," Edwards said. "There's still a rocket coming at you."

"I can take care of it."

"It's a Silkworm missile, targeted at the drone command center. It's thirty-four miles away and traveling 950 miles per hour. That means it'll be there in less than one minute. I don't think you'll be able to shoot it with the laser. Just run and save yourself!"

"No, it's too late."

"Then fucking do it! That Silkworm will be down your throat in thirty seconds."

Keyes shook her head. "Omar knew we might be able to stop the suicide bomber. That's why he ordered the Silkworm, too."

I sighted the X on the Silkworm as the count ticked to twenty seconds. "You have six shots left in that DE!" Edwards bellowed. "Shoot, damn it! Shoot!"

For some reason, I felt calm, as if I had complete control of the situation. I fired a shot.

"Fuck! A hundred yards short!" Edwards screamed.

I let go a volley of three shots as I moved the DE gun forward along the path of the missile.

"Short again!" Edwards yelled. "Two shots, seven seconds left!"

I quickly moved the DE forward and centered it on the Silkworm. This time, I had it.

Just as I pulled the trigger, the missile swerved to the left.

"You missed!" Edwards screamed, "Get out of there before it hits you!"

Keyes looked at me, tears welling in her eyes. "I'm sorry I got you into all this."

Without taking my eyes off the radar, I nodded and reassured her. "If my instincts are right, we're gonna' be just fine."

71

 TEN MILES FROM THE hospital, Herb Waters turned onto a scenic road that was little traveled except by weekend nature lovers. He'd thrown Keyes' cell phone out the window, in the event it had some type of tracking device.

With the Aston Martin's 510-horsepower engine, he could hit sixty in four seconds and quickly accelerate to speeds in excess of 100 miles per hour. He'd tested the Aston on country roads in America as well as on the Autobahn in Europe.

Cruising along now at 100 miles per hour, Waters smiled at the thought of Keyes and James being killed.

He then heard a whistling sound.

Waters looked left and right and then in his rearview mirrors. It was the missile. It wasn't headed for the hospital; it was coming at him. Hunching over the steering wheel, he pressed the accelerator to the floor. But the missile kept coming. A millisecond later, Waters and his car exploded.

Drone Control Center, Jackson City
3:38 pm

We heard a distant *pop*.

"I think that was the Silkworm missile blowing the shit out of Herb Waters."

Edwards' image immediately appeared on the screen. "What's happening? Did the hospital take a hit?"

Before answering, I quickly moved the cameras on the drone to the site of the last explosion. Then, I smiled and turned to Keyes. "That Rolex wasn't a watch. Not exactly. It was a beacon."

"Fa-*rok*," she whispered.

I looked at Edwards, and explained, "The Silkworm hit its target, which wasn't the hospital or the control center. It was a transmitting beacon inside a watch, which just happened to be in Herb Waters' Aston Martin."

"How do you know that?" Edwards asked.

I stared at Keyes sparkling eyes. "The watch kept getting slower. A good watch like that won't lose five minutes in a hundred years. So I knew somebody had fiddled with it. That, and it occurred to me that the casing was too big. Those jewels were on there to disguise the true size of a casing big enough to handle a transponder."

"That son of a bitch," Keyes hissed. "He put a marker in that watch!"

"He knew you'd find Waters and the drone center. That's why he gave you an extra day on your contract—so he could kill you and Waters at the same time."

"I'm too old for this stuff. My heart can't take it," Edwards said, as he wiped the moisture from his face. Every stitch of his clothing was soaked with sweat. He chuckled a little. "Dr. James, I can get you a job, replacing Charlie. I think I'll like working with you a lot better than that goddamn Waters!"

Edwards took a deep breath and held his hand to his headset for a moment. "We must catch Farok while he's in the area. Ms. Keyes, or whoever you are, where were you when you last saw Farok?"

"And Jorad Hormand," I interjected.

"Hormand? She saw Hormand?"

I looked at Keyes and asked, "You know, don't you?"

She just looked down.

I answered my own question. I looked at the monitor and said, "Farok and Hormand are one and the same. I searched Keyes' room when she was out and found a photograph. It was the same picture as the one circulated of Jorad Hormand. I'd seen it in several newspapers. Elizabeth, please tell us about that picture."

She hesitated before responding. "Omar likes masquerade

parties. I was with him a year ago when he tried to fool me one night with that disguise. A beard, heavy eyebrows, a plastic nose and cheeks, padded inserts for his stomach and butt, elevator shoes, the whole bit. It was so real. And, yes, the photo of Hormand is Omar in that disguise."

I wasn't surprised.

"I analyze the faces of people in photographs for a living, or at least I used to—before all this happened. Something was wrong with the face."

72

Watson Farm
Chapel Hill, North Carolina
4:01 p.m.

 THE LAUNCH AND THE flightpath of the Silkworm were plotted by Perkins' people, and within moments the UH-60 Blackhawk helicopters were in route to the Watson peanut farm.

The lead helicopter landed two miles from the farmhouse, where the terrorists were still celebrating the first strike on American soil by a Chinese Silkworm RBS-15 missile.

A second Blackhawk landed, and the U.S. combat teams assembled on the road, then moved in quietly to surround the farmhouse. Four squads of infantry breached the building at two doors. Just two captives were taken.

At the barn, where the Silkworm was launched, Michelle

hid now behind a farm tractor, with two of her soldiers. Five more missiles rested in rectangular cradles on a flatbed Mack truck, with camouflage paint.

Troops entered the barn within a minute of landing.

As they advanced, the two men of Michelle's group cautiously stepped out from behind the tractor with their hands out in front of them.

Michelle had other plans. "Fuck you!" she said as she leaned out from behind the tractor and fired her M-16.

The U.S. troops returned fire. It was five to one. The bullets from the U.S. guns flattened the tires of the tractor, blew off the seat and both fenders, and tore apart the fuel tank.

As Michelle lay dying, her final words were, "Allahu Akbar."

73

CIA Field Operations Command
Camp Peary, Virginia
7:00 p.m.

 Upon arriving at camp Peary, Keyes and I were taken immediately to a large conference room. There were no smiles or congratulations. We were debriefed by fifteen interrogators. All were serious and to the point. For more than an hour, we were bombarded with questions. Finally, the room fell silent, except for the sound of a small balding man in a general's uniform drumming his fingers on the table.

That has to be the "Perkins" who was Pete Harris' friend.

He stared at Keyes a full minute, his eyes steely as he studied her. He clasped his hands together and said icily, "Ms. Keyes, you are an illegal alien and you've been associated with known members of Al Qaeda and ISIS. As a terrorist, you pose a threat not only to the United States but also to the world. You are in trouble, big trouble, in this country. We show no mercy to terrorists. You face imprisonment for a long time, perhaps fifty years or more, depending on what charges we bring and your level of cooperation."

Keyes looked down and did not respond. I suppressed the urge to reach out to her.

"Do you have an answer to that?"

She looked into the eyes of her inquisitor. "But you haven't asked a question yet."

One member of the panel chuckled. The red-faced man pounded the desk with his fist and shouted, "Don't be coy with this panel! I demand you tell us all you know about Omar Farok and his terrorist organization!"

Keyes looked first at me and then at the floor. After a moment, she lifted her head and made eye contact with several of the panel members as she spoke. "Before today, Farok was pretty good to me. But like every other man in my life—with one exception." She glanced at me before continuing. "Like the others, Farok used me. And then he planned my death. I see now that he intended to kill me all along, from the time he programmed my phone until he gave me that watch."

The interrogators asked dozens of questions about Farok, but she remained mute. They quizzed me, but I knew as little about the man as the panel members did.

Finally, Keyes spoke. "I'll tell you everything if you give me and Dr. James full immunity from prosecution."

Perkins responded by pressing the intercom. "Please take our visitors to their quarters." Then, he turned to Keyes and me. "We'll break for dinner now. We'll summon you when we've made a decision."

Two soldiers arrived and led Keyes and me to separate rooms, where we spent the night.

CIA Field Operations Command
Camp Peary, Virginia
9:15 p.m.

During the closed session, the panel members discussed Keyes' involvement with the terrorists. She was just a courier. ISIS used her to find the drone site, nothing more. If Keyes, indeed, had the photographic memory that was attributed to her, she had a wealth of information to divulge.

Immunity was a good thing, if she would talk.

74

CIA Field Operations Command
Camp Peary, Virginia
7:00 a.m.

 THEY BROUGHT US BACK in. To my relief and surprise, they promised us full immunity. The only condition being that Keyes had to be perfectly forthright in disclosing information. If Keyes withheld something, or if she lied, the immunity would be revoked immediately.

I was taken to a private room while Keyes faced her interrogators.

She took a deep breath and began telling them all she knew. "Omar Farok planned this entire mission. He is the son of Ismael Muhammad Farok. He was born July, 17, 1970, in Damascus, Syria, and has five brothers and six sisters." She proceeded to give them the full names, birth dates and birthplaces, and even the last known addresses, complete with mail codes, of each member of the Farok family.

Keyes continued talking about Farok and his people and operation for almost an hour before the representative from the Advocate General's office in the room said, "Okay, okay, I'm satisfied with your knowledge and memory." He turned to the rest of panel. "If she keeps going like this, she gets immunity."

Camp Peary, Virginia
Three Days Later

THE CIA WASTED NO time putting Keyes' revelations to use. Over a three-day period, forty arrests were made in the United States, and eighteen terrorists were taken into custody in Saudi Arabia, Yemen, and The Sudan.

Keyes gave exact instructions on how to apprehend Farok. If he did what he'd done in the past, he would direct his Learjet to fly toward the West Coast and over the Canadian border, to escape to Asia.

The Canadian Air Force was put on alert. Radar picked up the aircraft right where Keyes said it would be, and six Canadian F-35 fighter planes intercepted it and forced a landing in Winnipeg.

But Farok was not on the plane, a mystery that not even Keyes could solve.

After three days of separate questioning, Keyes and I were

brought back together, and taken to the conference room. Perkins was there with two men I'd never seen before.

Perkins conducted the final debriefing. "Dr. James, I should inform you that Detective Harris' body was found in the trunk of a car in the hospital parking lot. The car was traced to a rental car company in Raleigh, North Carolina. The "official" report was that his beheading was the act of Middle Eastern terrorists whom Harris had gone looking for the night he was murdered."

"He was a friend of mine," I said.

"Mine, too."

Perkins looked down for a moment, then continued, with a smile growing on his face, "I should also inform you that the Jackson Police Department has dismissed the charges of murder in regards to Dr. Carey and Officer Wilson."

I smiled. I was incredibly relieved ... until Perkins continued. "Now, we found a Mercedes parked at an apartment complex with two bodies, both from the Congo. The gun that was in your possession killed both of the men." The general lifted up a plastic bag containing the Browning pistol. "Dr. James, your fingerprints are all over this gun."

He looked me in the eye. "With so many of your prints on this, I assume the pistol belongs to you."

"It was just—"

"I have some advice for you, Dr. James," he interrupted, silencing me with a stern look. "Be more careful with this in the future."

He handed me the gun. Only then did he smile.

The other two on the panel laughed.

Perkins turned his attention to Elizabeth. "Ms. Keyes, somehow, you entered the country illegally, probably in one of Farok's jets, but you never forged any false passports or financial or legal documents, or engaged in any fraudulent activities that we are aware of. Nor have you withheld information from this investigating body. In fact, your testimony has helped us greatly.

"I should tell you that coincident with the missile firing you witnessed, there was a car-bomb blast in Nice, France, yesterday, at one of the two residences owned by Herbert Waters. Three people were killed, including a woman identified as Mrs. Waters. There are no heirs listed in Mr. Waters' will other than several charities, which will receive a lot of money from foreign banks."

"But what about the hospital property?" I asked. "There's strong evidence to support Waters' ownership of Jackson City Hospital."

"We sifted through your notes, which were in Detective Harris' office. It does seem that through Waters' manipulation of the hospital bylaws, he is the legal owner of the hospital and all its entities. But the citizens of your city still think they own it, so unless Waters resurrects from the dead and lays claim to it, there's no one to challenge the city's ownership of the hospital."

He returned his attention to Keyes. "Ms. Keyes, you'll be our 'guest' in D.C. a while, until we've had access to all your information. If you continue to cooperate, we will allow you to return to Great Britain, your only place of apparent citizenship. Of course, we're fully aware that 'Keyes' is not your real birth name. But at this time, we don't have enough information to locate your actual birth certificate, if there ever was one.

"As we see it, ISIS attacked our country, and the two of you—an American physician and an English woman— fought valiantly to protect it. But the press won't get that part of the story. You will both be signing a mountain of confidentiality agreements. Prepare yourself for a case of writer's cramp."

Perkins smiled a little.

"The only thing the press needs to know is that American defense systems are operational and have outwitted ISIS." Perkins chuckled. "Maybe that will help us when our next budget goes for Congressional approval."

75

Jackson City
8:30 a.m.

 THE HOMELAND SECURITY AGENCY took complete control of the media coverage. They were ably assisted by the National Security Agency and the U.S. Air Force. We were sequestered at Camp Peary. All other witnesses to the events in Jackson City Hospital's Emergency Disaster bus were dead, except for Colonel Edwards. No ISIS group stepped up to claim responsibility for the attack, so the American news makers had the privilege of telling the story as it best benefited the interests of the United States, a real triumph in the war on terror.

The President of the United States received strong commendations for his actions in dealing with the terrorist attack in Jackson City. Interviews and polls of the American public showed overwhelming support in the handling of domestic terrorism with a great deal of praise for the administration, the performance of Congress, and the military complex, even though they had nothing to do with the outcome.

Throughout the next several days, foreign and domestic headlines alike read:

"America Thwarts ISIS Attack"

"North Carolina Hospital Bombed by Terrorists"

"American Military Captures Terrorist Missile Site Within Minutes of Attack"

"Terrorists Kill 5 at North Carolina Hospital"

"America Successful in Counter-Terrorist Strike"

No mention was made of either Dr. Scott James or Elizabeth Keyes.

76

ELIZABETH KEYES AND I said our goodbyes on the tarmac before she boarded the military transport to Washington. I held both her hands as we talked. She was headed to D.C. for an extended stay. Afterward, she would go home. She wanted to stay in America, and I wanted that, too, but immunity didn't stretch that far. She was forbidden from ever entering the United States again.

"Well, Scott, I can't say our time together was boring."

"Hard to debate that."

"Yeah." She looked down. A tear rolled down her cheek. Then she lifted her chin, wiped the tears from her eyes, and smiled. "I check my e-mail now and then. Who knows? Someday you might need someone with my special talents … if you ever get in trouble again."

"I don't know what your e-mail address is."

"I'm changing it. To the name and number you gave me

273

when you resurrected from death. Just remember, I'm a 'hot girl.' You'll figure it out."

I wanted to take her in my arms and kiss her, and she looked like she wanted the same. As we moved together, a federal officer stepped forward and pulled her away from me. "What will you do now?" Keyes called back to me, as she was led away.

"Water my orchids. I think I can resuscitate most of them. If I don't, they'll die."

"You can buy new ones."

"I don't want new ones. I've nurtured these for years. People think everything can be replaced. But that's not so. There's a value in things in which you invest your time, energy, and soul."

77

211 Pin Oak Drive
Jackson City, North Carolina

 IN OUR DIVORCE SETTLEMENT, Alicia made it clear that she wanted money, not responsibility. So I gave her a fat check and she gave me full custody of the kids. The kids and I moved into a small house close to the hospital, and we all tried to get our lives back on track.

My dream of a surgical practice was gone. I transferred all the orchids from the surgery center to my office at the hospital. The sunlight was too bright at my new office, so I bought special shades with my first paycheck.

The sale of my surgery center to a young plastic surgeon who'd come to the area from the University of Virginia erased all my debts. My new job as chief administrator of the Jackson City Hospital provided plenty of challenges in straightening out the huge financial mess, and returning the hospital to a workable, not-for-profit medical center.

For starters, I brought back free coffee for doctors and hospital employees.

Acknowledgments

To my mentor of the past three years, Richard Krevolin, who transformed a storyteller into a writer. Many times he had reason to think it was an impossible task, but due to his perseverance, this book finally can be printed. And he gives me hope that some of the dozens of other stories I have to tell might also be published.

My special thanks to Jeremy Fitzpatrick, a concerned citizen who discovered that the charter of a community hospital had been changed over the years, making it possible for the publicly funded hospital to be sold to a private entity, with potentially adverse financial consequences to the community. While it was not clear to him what the end result might have been at the time, the public opinion he generated in contacting local leaders and publishing a revealing letter to the editor of a local newspaper mysteriously seemed to stop the potential sale of the not-for-profit hospital. His revelations motivated me to investigate the matter further and to write this book.

To Steve Babitsky, whose SEAK courses for MD writers introduced me to other aspiring writers, accomplished authors, and publishers and opened the doors of book publishing.

To Paula Munier, who was kind to review my book and offer valuable suggestions about style that are included in it today.

To Lt. Col. Phillip Greasley, a retired Air Force flyer, who opened up to me the world of drones and military logistics and supplied references that allowed me to explore this fascinating subject.

Jim Williams, my medical illustrator for thirty years, who contributed to the original cover design.

Ana Magno, who created the original book cover and interior design.

To Colleen Sell, who did the edit on the original book.

To my son Glenn Jr., who has possessed mature writing skills since he was in the fifth grade—skills I will never have the talent to equal. But he encourages me to keep trying.

To my son Barclay, a computer geek, who kept me sane by pulling my story from the ashes of many computer crashes.

To John Hanson, who struggled through the reading of a half dozen of my earlier, primordial books and was kind enough not to criticize.

John Haslett and Annie Biggs, who were very helpful in directing the book to its final form.